THE PLOT AGAINST HIP HOP

THE PLOT AGAINST HIP HOP

A NOVEL BY
NELSON GEORGE

AKASHIC
BOOKS

This is a work of fiction. All names, characters, places, and incidents are the product of the author's imagination. Any resemblance to real events or persons, living or dead, is entirely coincidental.

Published by Akashic Books
©2011 Nelson George

ISBN-13: 978-1-61775-024-3
Library of Congress Control Number: 2011923105

Akashic Books
PO Box 1456
New York, NY 10009
info@akashicbooks.com
www.akashicbooks.com

CHAPTER 1
BIG PIMPIN'

Flashbulbs exploded into white light and the rapid click of cameras felt like an automatic weapon aimed at an innocent iris. D Hunter blinked and blinked again, trying not to appear as dizzy as he felt. This was no way to keep a rich MC safe.

"Jay! Jay, look over here!"

The camera posse shouted and the rap star, record mogul, and living breathing brand, with the hottest chick in the game wearing his ring, paused for the paparazzi, looking dap in a creamy white suit with matching powder-blue pocket square, tie, and trendy shades. He gave them his trademark sly smile and gracefully manipulated an unlit cigar like a mike. D hovered in the background, just out of camera range, his presence defining the edge of the frame.

Used to be that rap stars wore loose jeans, sideways Yankees caps, and a snarl. Bodyguarding was more about protecting them from themselves than keeping them safe from others. Wasn't it a decade ago that Jay was on the front page of the *Daily News*, accused of stabbing some kid for bootlegging his CDs? He was a public enemy spawned from the darkest reaches of the jungles of Crooklyn. Now Shawn Carter was a king of New York, and as mainstream as Sunday afternoon baseball.

Jay escaped the flashing cameras and walked toward the Boathouse, a scenic outdoor restaurant/event space off Fifth Avenue in Central Park that was the site of a huge charity bash this balmy summer eve. A

$1,000 ticket ($25,000 for a table), a nice tax deduction, a fat goody bag, and maybe a boat ride with a celebrity (who'd do the rowing) made this a well-heeled, upscale crowd.

D didn't know who or what they were raising money for, but he could see it must be something "in the hood" since hip hop heavies and Upper East Side swells were clinking glasses and recklessly eyeballing each other. Diddy. Andre 3000. Andre Harrell. Q-Tip. Russell Simmons was absent only because he was in St. Louis running one of his Hip-Hop Summits with Nelly. (In addition to raising awareness about the pitfalls that could affect black youths, the summit worked as soft promotion for their respective clothing lines.) Someone had resurrected Fonzworth Bentley for the affair, and he spun his umbrella and pursed his lips for the amusement of the blue-haired and pale-skinned.

D was outfitted in black, as was his custom, from his Hush Puppies loafers to his DKNY suit and Gap T-shirt. He settled in behind a table at the rear of the Boathouse, where Jay was parlaying with two fortyish Wall Street types. They were hyping him like crazy on a new energy drink, hoping to entice him to invest in and endorse their "can't miss" product. They wanted to call it Sparkle, suggesting a supple bling effect from the drink. "It's an aspirational beverage," one was saying earnestly, "like hip hop is an aspirational culture." One in every hundred cans would contain a piece of faux bling, while every ten thousandth would have a real tiny diamond. Jay listened politely, nodded, and took the odd puff on his now lit Cuban.

D stood back, amused by the two white pitchmen even as he wondered if he should buy some stock the next day. He enjoyed working for Jay cause the brother had cleaned up so nicely.

But his mind wandered. There were no threats in this space, no gunmen in the trees, no niggas sweating Jay for more than a handout or

a loan. The autograph seekers in this crowd were likely the offspring of
the rich, which meant D let them ask away, knowing somewhere down
the line their daddies might be useful to Jay. So, instead of staring down
the odd teenager with a napkin and Mont Blanc pen, D stood there
recalling his younger days when he'd go to the Apollo to see Doug E.
Fresh or Rakim headline or to Union Square where kids slipped razor
blades under their tongues, listened to Red Alert spin, and scoped for
vics. He listened to the "Old School at Noon" shows on the local hip
hop stations religiously, loving when a gem from the Classical Two or
the Treacherous Three was dropped. PE and BDP and De La were the
stuff that had animated his life when he was young. Now hip hop was
big business for him, just like it was for everyone who made records.

His company, D Security, made its monthly nut securing starlets,
MCs, A-list events, and the odd after-hours party. In large part it was the
remaining glamour of the rap game that kept his little business afloat,
though these brothers tended to pay slower than, say, Miley Cyrus's
people. D absently touched the insignia pin on his lapel. It was the only
bit of light on his body and it served as an identifier for his employees.
A gold *D* against a royal-blue background. Against the advice of many,
he'd kept the pin clear of diamonds. For D the button was a classic look,
like Adidas' white shell–toe sneaker and the Yankees' white-on-blue
NY. He wasn't gonna change D Security's logo like some bad athletic
team switching colors to distract fans from their lousy record.

D gazed around the Boathouse, glanced over to where DJ Beverly
Bond played the latest hip hop/R&B fusion from a cute, faceless girl
group, and thought of the parties in the park and underground clubs
and mad passion that had made benefits like this possible, parties where
very wealthy white folk conspired with merely rich black folk to turn
that energy into lucrative product. It was, D decided, the American

Dream manifest. In God we trust—in cash we lust.

D glanced at his watch. In a bit Jay would bore of the business pitches and head over to the studio where his latest mentee, a kid from Baltimore who had a crunk attitude and old-school skills, was laying down some tracks. Jay would probably stay most of the night, listening to how it was going down and adding his very important two cents. It was cool to see the vet work with this kid, but D wouldn't have to stay that long. One of his men would roll by for overnight duty and D would slide over to his office in Soho to do some paperwork. The accountant was coming tomorrow and he had to go over the books. Thank you, hip hop, he thought. I owe you one.

CHAPTER 2
DEAD HOMIEZ

D kept his office so dark some people called it his dungeon. Black walls. Burnished-ebony wood furniture. No bright colors. Nothing white save the printouts from his laptop, the envelopes containing bills that filled his inbox, and the skin of an occasional visitor. There was one gold record on his wall. It was for Public Enemy's *It Takes a Nation of Millions*, a gift from an old friend who had been cleaning out his house in Jersey and passed it on. The office was as big as a good-sized bathroom in a four-star hotel.

D Security's other room was a fairly large meeting space dominated by a long conference table. Next to it was a setup to recharge walkie batteries, a coffee machine, and a locker where employees stored snacks, clothes, and brass knuckles.

D was writing an e-mail to Russell Simmons about handling security for his next Diamond Empowerment event when he heard a bump against the front door. He went into the little lobby—really just a waiting room with two metal chairs and a framed vintage Run-D.M.C. poster—and opened the door.

Slumped at the foot of the door, wearing a bloody beige trench coat and a blue Yankees cap, was the music critic Dwayne Robinson. Blood oozed from wounds to his chest and arms, and there was a nasty slice to his right cheek. D reached down and placed his hand against his friend's brown skin, hoping he could somehow slow the flow of blood from his neck. Dwayne's eyes flickered for a moment and he mumbled, "D?"

"Yeah, man. Tell me who did this."

"Remix. It's all a remix."

"What?"

"Biggie was right."

"About what?"

"It was all a dream."

There was no more. No more light. No more words. No more Dwayne Robinson. His soul had departed. All that was left in D's hands were clothes smeared with crimson spots and a body soon to grow cold.

D had seen death up close way too often to panic in its presence. In fact, it had once been almost as constant to him as air, marking his childhood with ghoulish benchmarks. But that was back in Browns-ville, Brooklyn, a lost neighborhood where the streets were saturated with generation after generation of ghetto blood. No one had deserved to die, not his friends, not his brothers. No one who grew up in the Ville was surprised by death. But Dwayne Robinson was a middle-aged black intellectual. A music critic. An author. Why would anyone slash a man like that with a box cutter in goddamn Soho?

D lifted up Dwayne's bloody palm and his eyes began to water. He was rising to go call the cops when he noticed a square black object clutched in Dwayne's lifeless right hand. Haven't seen one of those in years, he thought. It was a black plastic TDK audio cassette, like the kind he'd played a million times on his old Panasonic boom box. It looked ancient.

D knew this was now crime scene evidence but nevertheless pried the tape from Dwayne's stiffening fingers. Stuck to the side of it was a yellowed label scrawled with *Harlem World Battle*. D went back into his office and dialed 911, all the while squeezing the TDK tape in his bloody hand. Looked around his office and realized he hadn't owned a cassette player in years. That was another era. High-top fades. Painter's caps. Four-finger rings. Dapper Dan's Gucci knockoffs. Dwayne Robinson's era. *Village Voice* reviews. Critical commentaries. Nationalist rhetoric. All of it "out of here" like that KRS-One rhyme.

A red-eyed D was listening to Rakim's "Lyrics of Fury" on his iPod when the two patrolmen arrived.

CHAPTER 3
LYRICS OF FURY

I own *The Relentless Beat* myself," Fly Ty said as he laid out the crime scene photos on his cluttered NYPD desk. "Man, this hurts me too. He was one of the few motherfuckers who cared to know the history of our music . . . though he did spend too much time trying to justify that rap shit to suit me." Fly Ty, a.k.a. Detective Tyrone Williams, stood with his hands on the sides of his blue pin-striped suit. His white shirt was crisp and his blue tie was tasteful. His gray hair was cut short and his sideburns just long enough to let you know why everyone called him Fly Ty. Underneath that suit was a fit body whose age was only betrayed by a small, soft pouch of flesh just below his belly. Otherwise Fly Ty looked like he could still fit in a patrolman's uniform and shame every rookie in his precinct.

While D stared mournfully at the photos of the late author, the detective asked if he had moved the body.

"Just touched his neck, trying to stop the bleeding, and took that tape out of his hand. But obviously he wasn't attacked in my hallway."

"Nope," Fly Ty agreed as he sat down behind his desk, smoothed out his tie, and looked up at D. The two men had met when D was a ten-year-old and Ty was the best-dressed flatfoot walking the mean streets of Brownsville. Now the detective picked up a file and read, *"Dwayne Robinson was attacked on Crosby, near Prince, right behind the Dean & Deluca delivery door. A Mexican worker and a yoga instructor described the attackers as two young men—one definitely black, about nineteen, and the other either Latino or light-skinned black. Both slim and about six feet. Both wearing red doo rags and tracksuits. They were seen getting into—"*

"What? A red Range Rover?"

"No. A dark-colored SUV driven by another man, but the two witnesses differ as to his racial background."

"At least they spared us a red car."

"Who's *they?*"

"The motherfuckers determined to make it look like some Bloods stabbed my man in a gang initiation."

"Aside from the location," Fly Ty suggested, "that's what it looks like."

To which D said, "Bullshit," loud enough that two white detectives glanced over, wondering who had the balls to curse in the direction of the formidable veteran.

"C'mon, Fly Ty, this shit happens in the hood, not Soho. Kids like that don't drive into white neighborhoods in Manhattan to do this."

"Relax," Fly Ty said. "These kinds of stabbings do happen on the Upper West Side near MLK High and in Union Square near Washington Irving High."

"But there's no high school in Soho—unless they're now holding remedial reading classes in the back of D&D."

The two men fell silent for a moment. D picked up one of the photos and looked at Dwayne's neck and saw how deep the wound was. "It's too easy, Fly Ty. If it's Bloods, it's a random attack. Easy to explain. Easy to file away."

"You should teach Police Academy courses since you seem to know so damn much," Fly Ty replied, then gathered another file from his desk. "Got most of this off Google. *Dwayne Robinson. Fifty. Music critic/*

historian. Resides in Montclair, New Jersey. Wife: Danielle. Published a number of books. Taught journalism at Columbia J School. Through the years he wrote some nasty reviews of some famous folks. Pissed off quite a few people. But bad reviews are rarely motives for murder. No gambling debts. No drug use. No serious affairs, though there were rumors he might have strayed with a coed or two." He set the file down. "Let's say it was a hit, D. Why would someone pay two knuckleheads to wet up the good professor?"

D's answer was, "Let's listen to the tape."

The interrogation room smelled of body odor and stale cologne, and had that gray-green institutional color scheme. It was a strange place to listen to the rhymes of Moe Dee and Busy Bee blasting out of an ancient boom box that someone had found in the evidence room.

To Fly Ty this was typical "young nigga gibberish."

To D it was a great freestyle battle. "Really legendary. They did this at the Harlem World Disco on the corner of Lenox and 116th Street, across from Malcolm's mosque."

"Nice black history moment, D. What's it got to do with Robinson's death?"

D frowned, not sure what to say.

Fly Ty opened another file and quickly scanned it. "His wife said he came into the city to have drinks with his editor, which has been confirmed. He told Ms. Wolfe that he was working on a memoir/revisionist hip hop history. That meeting ended about eight p.m. He ended up at your door around ten-thirty. Two and a half hours. That's plenty of time for a man to get in trouble in New York City."

D stopped the tape, fast-forwarded to the end, flipped it over, and pressed play. No more MC battle. A hip hop beat filled the room and two voices could barely be heard underneath. "That's Dwayne right there," D said. "I don't recognize the other one. You gonna send this to CSI?"

Fly Ty sighed at the now all-too-common question. "When I get it back from the sound lab, maybe we'll be able to identify the other voice."

"So," D wondered, "how much time you gonna put into this?"

"We'll see. The antigang task force will be brought in. They'll probably wanna talk to you."

"But what about you? You're a top detective. If you make it a priority, it'll be one."

"Look," Fly Ty answered, "despite what you might have heard about crime dropping in New York, we get dead bodies every day. I got three other cases in my lap. He's your friend. That means something to me. But I ain't dropping everything for this. At least not without more to go on."

After his unsatisfying afternoon with Fly Ty, D walked down Crosby, from Howard to the back of Dean & Deluca on Prince, where he turned west to Broadway, striding through the crowds exiting the R station and the Armani Exchange. He passed through shoppers and yogis and delivery boys into his building, and then went up the elevator to his office on the tenth floor of 580 Broadway. He stood in front of the door with keys in hand, staring down for a moment at where the janitor had mopped up the blood, before entering.

The stench of disinfectant filled the office as D pulled out his hardcover edition of *The Relentless Beat*. In the hierarchy of music literature it wasn't quite *Blues People*, *Mystery Train*, or *The Death of Rhythm & Blues*. But Dwayne Robinson's book was still taught at a lot of colleges and he had continued to lecture from it every Black History Month. He had inscribed this copy to the bodyguard: *My man D. Keep on dreamin'.*

D closed the book and slid out his BlackBerry. A few years back he'd stopped three teenagers from lighting a homeless man on fire at the Canal Street A station. He'd later befriended one of the kids and used him for odd jobs from time to time. Now he called Ray Ray.

"Two guys who looked like Bloods stabbed a friend of mine to death in Soho the other night."

"Bloods in Soho? Hmmm. That's some new shit."

"Yeah, well, I need to find them. They drove off in a Range Rover." D gave the young man the details he knew about what they looked like.

Ray Ray said, "You know this ain't the Mafia. It's not like it's one family. Niggas be freelancing all over the place."

"I'll give you $200 for your time and another $800 if you find out something useful."

"Well," Ray Ray responded, "I better make myself useful."

CHAPTER 4
NEVER SEEN A MAN CRY
UNTIL I SEEN A MAN DIE

The cuts on Dwayne's neck and face were sealed for the funeral and the morticians even managed to put on his trademark lopsided grin so that the writer would face eternity with that same mischievous look that those who knew him best so treasured. The local Baptist church on Orange was filled with a who's-who of the folks Dwayne had written about so eloquently—Spike Lee, Anita Baker, Whitney Houston, Chuck D, Prince, Vernon Reid, and so many others. Many of his subjects had become friends.

With all this black pop royalty at the funeral, there was one person conspicuous by his absence. Walter Gibbs had known Dwayne since both were young hustling dudes trying to make it in the intense, innovative New York of the early 1980s. Dwayne had chronicled his parties and profiled the acts he managed. Walter had become rich; Dwayne had become respected. A huge wreath with Gibbs's name on it at the funeral parlor led several mourners to wonder aloud, "Where the fuck is Gibbs?" D didn't speculate. He just filed the fact away.

Dwayne had been one of those people who everybody knew, who connected people like spokes on a wheel. D was younger than most of the artists there and yet he'd been touched by Dwayne Robinson too. Russell Simmons, who'd known Dwayne well since they first met years back at a roller disco in Queens, gave an amusing eulogy about their adventures in rap's formative years. Anita Baker, Dwayne's favorite singer, performed "No One in the World," a song not ideally suited for a funeral but one Dwayne's wife said he would have wanted.

The casket wasn't too heavy. D had been the pallbearer in many previous funerals, so he'd come to appreciate a light corpse, no matter how heartless that was. Dwayne's spirit, his essence, had been taken by a killer or killers unknown. What was inside the box that D helped carry meant nothing compared to the collective memory of what Dwayne had achieved during his unexpectedly brief life.

At one point D sat down in the living room of the Robinson's comfy three-story home with a plate in his lap, listening more than talking as people dined on soul food and sweet-potato pie and reminisced about Dwayne and the world that shaped him. D soon found himself, quite happily, squeezed into a corner with Grandmaster Flash and Kool Moe Dee talking about a rap tour circa 1984. He asked if Moe had any idea why Dwayne was carrying a copy of his famous battle during his last night on earth.

"I wish I knew," Moe said. "I wish I knew. We'd stayed in contact over the years. Any time he did a reading or had an event in Los Angeles, he'd invite me. We'd talk about the '80s. In fact, he seemed very interested in the period around '88, '89. Talked about doing a book. Guess we'll never know what he was up to."

Danielle Robinson, a petite woman whose graying hair contrasted with bright, youthful black eyes, came over and offered D another plate. He felt awkward about being the last person to see her husband alive; he was embarrassed in her presence. When he told her he was already full, Danielle reached out and took his large hands in her slender fingers. "My husband really liked you," she said.

"Oh," he replied, fumbling for words, "he was great to me. Like a big brother who made sure you listened to all the right records and read all the right books."

"Thank you for trying to save him."

Again D struggled in response, making sounds and not syllables before falling into silence and feeling a tear drop from one eye. Suddenly the little woman had her arms around the waist of the massive man, offering comforting words as he wept. In her kindness, Danielle allowed D to go upstairs, away from the eyes of those gathered in the living room, to a guest bathroom on the second floor where he could wash his face and regain his composure. Perhaps, he thought, I'm not as used to death as I tell myself.

D was standing at the top of the landing when he noticed more stairs leading to the attic where Dwayne kept his office. He'd been up there once to do an interview about the trials of bodyguarding rap stars for a script the writer had been working on. D knew it would be an intrusion, maybe a touch disrespectful, but he couldn't help himself. He headed up the stairs.

A large black-and-white photo of a screaming Otis Redding in a sharkskin suit was taped to the door. The singer had been a favorite of Dwayne's mother, and D's mother had liked him too—though she was more of the Teddy Pendergrass generation of black-love men. D would have preferred to linger on that convergence of taste, but opening the door to Dwayne's office welcomed him to a harsh new reality.

The room was a shambles. Manuscript pages strewn across the floor. An old mahogany desk overturned. CDs and books were sliding onto the floor from a ceiling-high bookcase. Judging by the white cords still plugged into outlets, Dwayne's computers had been removed. Ironically, the framed pictures on the wall looked untouched: Dwayne with Anita Baker, with Jimmy Jam and Terry Lewis, with Eazy-E, with Q-Tip.

D stared at the disarray and the photos and thought he was gonna tear up again, but he pushed the feeling back down. It was enough having to tell Danielle her house had been broken into during her husband's funeral. He wasn't going to do it looking like a whiny bitch.

Danielle waited until most of the guests had left before calling the police.

"This is terrible," she said.

D sat silent, unsure for a moment what to say on a day that had turned from very sad to horrible. "Was he working on a book?"

"Yes. He was calling it *The Plot Against Hip Hop*."

"Hell of a title."

"I thought so too. I thought it sounded melodramatic. But he kept telling me it was his best book yet. The one he'd be remembered for. And now this."

D held Danielle Robinson, feeling her shake as she endured another loss, another violation of her world. "It was all a dream." That's what D said.

The Montclair police were remarkably nice. One of the patrolmen told D that Dwayne had gotten name recording artists to perform at charitable events in the area over the years and was extremely well liked in town. D gave the cop, a brother named Fred Harris, his card and asked him to let him know what they found. He also made sure he passed on Fly Ty's number since this robbery made Dwayne's murder clearly more than a gang initiation. Dwayne had died for "something." It wasn't random. Not at all.

When Fred asked about getting some club security in the city for extra dollars, D knew he had a useful new friend.

On the way back to Manhattan, D mulled over the latest turn in

Dwayne Robinson's murder and took some stock of his own life. D often felt like his existence had been just a series of unsolved mysteries. He didn't know where his father was; he didn't know why his brothers had been shot; he didn't understand why God had allowed him to contract the HIV virus. But Dwayne's death? There was an answer to that. It was something he could solve, something he could know the truth about.

CHAPTER 5
LOOKIN' FOR THE PERFECT BEAT

D hadn't picked up Dwayne Robinson's *The Relentless Beat* since he'd first met the author in the mid-'90s when Dwayne had already begun his long, slow retirement from covering music full-time for a variety of publications. Back then there were enough music magazines that, if you hustled, you could eke out a living from record and concert reviews, and celebrity profiles.

Dwayne had got out just in time, before the Internet destroyed the print music mags and created a legion of nonpaying blogs where anyone could spew opinions and few were paid anything approaching a living wage. At the beginning of their relationship it was Dwayne who'd treated for long lunches, where he schooled D on the differences between the soul songs of Philly, Detroit, Chicago, and Memphis. In the last few years it was D who picked up the check for dinner while he kept the middle-aged writer hip to the Lil's and Yung's of contemporary rap.

Now D sat in the Starbucks nearest his Seventh Avenue apartment, leafing through *The Relentless Beat* to mourn his friend and search for some connection between his greatest work and his murder. The book had been published at the height of the golden age of New York hip hop, a time that now seemed utopian in its optimism. There was no doubt in Dwayne's mind that Chuck D and KRS-One were street prophets, that Rakim and Kane were true urban poets, and that talents like LL Cool J and rival Kool Moe Dee were champs of bodacious boasting. Flow, articulation, and sticking to theme were celebrated; freestyle ciphers in narrow ghetto hallways were crucibles of fire.

Dwayne's central idea was that the radical intellectual fire, passionate one-upsmanship, and straight-up virility of hip hop's greatest MCs had made them—and not the R&B singers of that era—the true inheritors of the masculine mantle of soul. The author was quite disdainful of the nonthreatening, jheri curl–wearing, kinda bisexual generation of singers who filled the playlist of urban contemporary radio.

To a great degree *The Relentless Beat* tossed much of the black pop that was emanating from the major West Coast labels under a fast-moving tour bus. Only the work of a few producers (Quincy Jones, Leon Sylvers), record label heads (Solar's Dick Griffey, Total Experience's Lonnie Simmons), and a couple of power brokers (Clarence Avant, Amos Pilgrim) elicited any praise from the New York–centric journalist. Dwayne had clearly turned in his manuscript before he heard NWA's "Straight Outta Compton" and the gangs of South Central changed the West Coast game forever.

As engaging as *The Relentless Beat* remained, it was a powerful document that offered no clues or secret codes to suggest who might have stabbed its author to death half a lifetime later.

CHAPTER 6
AMERIKKKA'S MOST WANTED

For days after the funeral D tried to set up a meeting with Walter Gibbs. He called, e-mailed, and text messaged, but Gibbs was either traveling or in a conference, or just plain unavailable. He was never told Gibbs didn't wanna talk to him. Nor was his outreach ever unreturned. The replies were always very polite. Never "no way" they'd meet or "Don't call again." More like, "Mr. Gibbs will return your call at his earliest convenience." It was the classiest brush-off D had ever experienced.

Despite the stonewall, D kept trying. What else was there to do? Fly Ty had nothing to report and was gruff when asked about the investigation, especially the audio tape. The gang guys had called once, spoke very perfunctorily, and hadn't called back. Ray Ray was asking around but couldn't be too aggressive. There were so many Bloods and so much blood. Felt like a dead end indeed.

So when D got a call from Walter Gibbs's office, he was as surprised as he was pleased. However, the invitation that followed was not to talk about Dwayne or death or hip hop. Gibbs had been an early hip hop manager and an indie label head during the breakthrough '80s. In the '90s he secured a distribution deal with a major label, then bought a fancy house in the Hollywood Hills to be closer to TV and film. He executive produced a couple of rap soundtracks for urban movies and got his feet wet as an associate producer on one of Wesley Snipes's action flicks. Gibbs saw his future on celluloid.

Then one day at the posh Polo Lounge in Beverly Hills, Gibbs's life changed. He was supposed to meet a white ingénue for lunch and maybe a quickie at her nearby condo. On his way over he spotted a table with Lionel Richie, two fine-ass Filipinas, and a balding Jewish man dressed in a pink and white sweater, white pants, rakish shades, and a deep Palm Springs tan. Morgie, a.k.a. Samuel Morgenstern, was in the leisurewear business. He'd met Lionel playing golf at an LA country club and they'd become fast friends, meeting occasionally for drinks and female company at this old Hollywood haunt.

Gibbs had quickly forgotten about his date, drawn to the black pop-star power, the Asian beauties, and, most fatefully, Morgie's business acumen. Turned out Morgie was raised in the same Brooklyn ghetto that had spawned Gibbs—albeit four decades earlier. Morgie's family had owned two retail outlets in that hood. By the time they met that afternoon at the Polo Lounge, Morgie owned three hundred clothing stores in various ghettos throughout the Northeast, but was trying to figure out the new urban buyer. Clearly Lionel Richie wasn't the person to ask, but Morgie immediately saw Gibbs as a kindred BK salesman.

Out of that chance meeting a partnership was born. Taking all he'd learned in the hip hop biz and applying it to Morgie's stores, Gibbs transformed them into new jack emporiums that sold every hot item an urban consumer could want (including a couple of spots that sold some herb out the back). Gibbs was so effective that Morgie even gave the young black man a (small) piece of the business. With that as his calling card, Gibbs began a consulting firm with clients from Coke to Cadillac, all of whom wanted to tap the "urban" market (and the white kids who followed its lead).

And it was this business that got D invited to Gibbs's swanky lower-Fifth Avenue office. D rolled into the large glass-enclosed conference room and shook hands with various reps from the maker of Lee jeans. They had designed a new straight-legged dungaree aimed at the black/Hispanic/Asian rebel. This particular meeting was focused on coordinating the details of a party to launch the jeans at Macy's. Lots of hip hop celebs would be in effect, along with some basketball players, video vixens, and various scenesters. D was being brought in to handle security, which would be a well-paying gig.

Gibbs greeted him graciously when he entered but, with seven other folks in the room, D didn't mention Dwayne or his funeral. Near the end of the meeting a luscious Latina came into the conference room and whispered to Gibbs. He nodded, mumbled "Yeah," and then excused himself. D wanted to say, *Stop! Don't duck me anymore, motherfucker!* But he knew that wasn't the move. When Gibbs disappeared out the door D was determined to find his personal office and, if he had to, barge in and demand an audience.

Thankfully all that drama wasn't necessary. As the meeting broke up that same Latina, about twenty-seven with thick black hair, a little round in the waist, but still easy on the eyes, came over to D. "Mr. Hunter, Mr. Gibbs wonders if you had a moment."

In contrast to the bright, sleek, modernist design of the rest of the office, Gibbs's space was dimly lit and a little smoky. The ashtray on his desk held two dead cigars with one still smoldering. Sharing the desk with the tray were stacks of reports full of multicolored graphs and bullet points. Next to them was a D.M.C. doll, one of a Japanese line of collectibles built around famous hip hop figures. The rest of the desk was covered in various devices—BlackBerry, Sony Playstation, iPod, and a futuristic thing D couldn't place.

He had a couple minutes to contemplate Gibbs's desk since the mogul wasn't actually there yet. Well, D thought, *I did make it into* the dude's office. At least I did that. To kill time between sips of the Evian that the Latina had generously handed him, D practiced a trick Dwayne had told him about back in the day. D began trying to read Gibbs's files upside down. You couldn't get the small print but a log line or caption here or there could yield a nugget of useful info.

From what D could see, most of the reports were marketing surveys of "urban buying habits" tied to "embedded brand desire." It was the gobbledygook of psychological selling, something D had often encountered in meetings with people trying to move sneakers, video games, and liquor. D didn't understand much about it, though he knew that anyone who talked that talk could squeeze a living out of corporations from here to hell and back. Gibbs had gone from selling records out of the backs of cars to selling digital dreams to lifestyle companies and the big Walmart brand.

D was gazing at an upside-down graph of red, blue, and green lines when Gibbs walked in wearing a white shirt, jeans, and a diamond in each earlobe. "Sorry about the wait, D," he began after a handshake and a polite hug. "I had to change for a meeting I have in fifteen minutes. But I wanted to make sure I spoke to you before I left." In that one bit of dialogue Gibbs had put a time limit on their conversation, while also acknowledging the need to speak. D dove right in.

"As you probably know, I was the last person Dwayne Robinson spoke to before he died."

"Yeah, I read that."

"The police have no leads and are treating this as a Bloods initiation. Simple as that."

"But you think his last words mean something. A clue to who did it."

"Maybe more like *why* it happened. At least I hope they do."

"I've thought a lot about it since I read that stuff in the papers. It's funny cause I never thought Dwayne was a huge Biggie fan, so for him to reference the dude at that moment, it had to be about more than a record."

"What's your guess?"

"I hate to say this, but I don't know that I have a guess. To be honest, these last few years Dwayne and I haven't been close. I mean, if I ran into him it was all love on my part. But we had some major differences over the direction of my life."

"I don't wanna get all up in your business, but were the differences things that, you know, reflected his state of mind?"

"Well, he was one of the few people I knew from back in the day who didn't think I'd sold out. No. He thought we'd been sold out."

"*We'd?*"

"Yeah, like everyone who was in the hip hop game had been talked out of being rebels and just handed the culture over to corporate America for chump change."

"You know he was writing a book titled *The Plot Against Hip Hop*."

"That's strange to me." Gibbs paused now, his face revealing both anger and amusement. "How a man who'd seen how we'd all pushed and shoved this street culture into an industry could think that one force or person could control its direction—well, that idea just tripped me out. These niggas are so hard-headed you can barely get two MCs to do a tour together without someone shooting someone backstage. In fact, niggas are, by definition, antiorganization. That's why I do what I do now. I can't be around fools who shoot each other over diamonds. Anyway, when Dwayne came up with all this mess I thought he was joking, but he meant it. Over time that made things a little tense between us. Instead of a normal conversation, every time I saw Dwayne things got a little crazy."

"I don't remember him acting that way."

"Well, D, you didn't know him as well or for as long as I did. No disrespect. It's just the truth."

"Okay," D said after a long beat. He suddenly felt like it was time for him to go.

"Believe me," Gibbs continued with some softness, "I know you feel obligated to look into Dwayne's murder. I'm glad someone aside from NYPD is. You know that KRS-One song 'Kill a Rapper'? He put it out there with Marley Marl. He says the best method to get away with murder is to kill a rapper. Damned if Dwayne didn't die an MC's death."

"Yeah." D stood up. "I guess you're right." He didn't know what else to ask. He was sure there was more to find out, but he felt a little intimidated and outclassed by Gibbs and now just wanted to leave as bad as he had wanted in. "Thanks for your time, man. And I'm very happy to be working with your company on this event."

Gibbs stood up behind his desk. "Shit," he said, "talking about Dwayne, well, it was good for me. I know you know I didn't go to the funeral. I know that was fucked up. I don't have an excuse. He came to my first parties, back before I was even in the hip hop game and was promoting R&B singers. We went through a lot together." For the first time in their conversation Gibbs looked emotional. He picked up one of the marketing reports from his desk. "This is funny. The first time I dipped my toe in the corporate game, it was because of him. I helped do research for a survey of the hip hop market that he was writing for some marketing company. Shit, that's what I do now 24/7/365. Things do change."

"You remember the name of the survey?"

"It was probably something like 'Understanding the Hip Hop Market: Its Aspirations, Its Potential.'" Gibbs laughed. "I don't know the name. I do remember I got paid by this company called Sawyer. Dwayne worked hard on that thing; I guess it was my first sellout move, huh? But you can't really sell out in hip hop. It was all about buying in, in the first place."

At that moment the lovely Latina popped her head in. Time for Gibbs to go. Next meeting.

D asked, "You think you have a copy of it?"

"Oh no. That was what, twenty or so years ago. Besides, that report would be as outdated as an MC Shan twelve-inch."

D gave the luscious Latina a lingering glance as he left Gibbs's office, hoping he'd get a chance to see her again at the Macy's event. Absorbing her thick hair and light brown skin—she was probably Dominican, he thought—briefly distracted him from the uncomfortable conversation he'd just had with her boss. He hadn't really learned much. Dwayne was probably the least "crazy" man he'd known. Maybe he'd become overzealous when talking about his books, but "crazy" seemed the word of a man who wasn't used to having his worldview questioned.

Was the Sawyer marketing survey a clue? Probably not. But in a world where almost anything could be found somewhere on the net, D was sure he could run down a copy. It might be fun to read prognostications about hip hop written back in the '80s. How close could they have come to predicting this future?

CHAPTER 7
YOU MUST LEARN

Back at his office with his Apple Pro computer radiating a blue glow upon his face, D contemplated his search options. If Dwayne Robinson was still alive he'd have been the first person D would have called. He'd done the next best thing and called Dwayne's wife. Danielle said the Sawyer report sounded vaguely familiar, but when she looked through the bibliography of Dwayne's work she'd been compiling, it wasn't there. Perhaps a copy had been amongst the papers in his ransacked attic office.

But no sign of it now. Danielle wasn't surprised that Gibbs knew of it and she didn't. She'd always seen the talent-manager-turned-marketing-guru as a bad influence on her husband. "When Dwayne did anything with Gibbs, especially in the years before were we married, he was usually not too anxious to tell me about it," she had said. "We had a very serious breakup years before we reconnected and Gibbs played a role in that. It's probably one of the reasons he didn't come to the funeral. It was an unspoken thing between us all."

D took all that in. Maybe it explained Gibbs's somewhat defensive behavior during their talk. Still, no luck in tracing the Sawyer report. After speaking to Danielle, D got on the phone to some editors at *Source* and *Vibe*, but they were clueless when it came to anything that happened before 1992. He tried a couple of hip hop academics but they were worthless on the report too.

So now D did what he usually dreaded—he entered hip hop cyber-space. Aside from checking out ESPN.com and NBA.com, D wasn't very interested in the Internet. Normally he would have asked his assistant or one of his net-addicted staffers to surf around for him. But he'd decided not to get any of his staff involved with his private investigation into Dwayne's death. Sure, they were loyal to him, but chasing down unsolved murders wasn't like breaking up bar fights or keeping screaming groupies behind barricades. Dwayne's death was his burden and was best kept private.

So there he was on AllHipHop.com, Okayplayer.com, GlobalGrind.com, and on and on, typing *Sawyer report* into search engines, querying editors, and asking online communities if anybody had heard of it. From distant corners of the hip hop world, bits of reconnaissance floated in: Davey D from the Bay Area had heard tell of it in the early '90s but he'd never seen a copy; some young head on MurderDog.com had a cousin who had found a copy while researching his dissertation, but that relative had been shot dead while buying herb; a kid in Amsterdam said his father had worked on it but Pops didn't have a copy.

Twenty pages in on Google, D came across a site called Hiphop-cointelpro.com. *COINTELPRO* had been the FBI's code name for its various nefarious strategies to undermine the efforts of the Black Panthers, the U.S. Organization, and other nationalist groups to organize the black masses in the '50s and '60s. Character assassination, espionage, and straight-up murder were all coordinated by J. Edgar Hoover's men in a tragically successful campaign to send big Afro-wearing leaders into jail, exile, insanity, or the grave.

There had been scattered signs of law enforcement monitoring hip hop throughout its short history. A police letter was once sent around the country warning local authorities about the danger of letting NWA perform in their jurisdictions. Rappers such as Busta Rhymes, who'd refused to cooperate in murder investigations, were regularly pulled over and searched by aggressive patrolmen in what looked like systematic harassment. But nothing in the hip hop era came close to Hoover's campaign of terror. The bottom line: for all their posturing as important voices of the people, MCs hadn't been dangerous to the system since the early '90s. These days everybody was complacently capitalistic and proud of it. No need to waste government money on diamond-studded entertainers, who were more nuisances than threats, when there were terrorist sand niggas for the feds to clock.

Yet Hiphopcointelpro.com was full of every conspiracy theory you could imagine. Biggie and Tupac were killed by elements of LAPD's rogue Rampart Division. Bootlegged rap CDs were being used to fund CIA counterterror operations in the Caribbean. AIDS in Africa was a long-term strategy to clear large parcels of land for European and Chinese business interests. One story went all the way back to the KKK owning the company that made Troop jackets when they became popular urban gear. Like Fox News, Hiphopcointelpro.com sold paranoia and was damned entertaining in doing so. One section of its home page read:

> Many people cannot fathom just how deep this war against the rising consciousness in the music went (and is still going). Military/intelligence-directed psychological operations in the form of gangsta rap. Chemical warfare (crack, malt liquor, PCP, heroin) to destabilize and commit genocide in targeted communities. Strategic biological warfare known as AIDS. The development, funding, and coopting of pseudogangs (Crips, Bloods, Latin Kings) with the top leadership and U.S. intelligence. The strategic funneling of arms throughout the African-American community by military intelligence.

> *The major record labels are all controlled by the same elite of people, who run their businesses through the occult and are the heads of secret societies like the Freemasons and Illuminati. For a musician to sign with one of these labels, you have to be willing to work toward the agenda, which is to eventually obtain total control over the world population. This doesn't mean that all artists signed are aware of the agenda, but they are tied to the rules of the industry. These artists become mind-control victims of a programmer or handler (usually a manager or attorney).*

One of D's favorite images on the site was a Rose Garden pic of President Ronald Reagan and Vice President George H.W. Bush with the caption, *The Real Godfathers of Crack & Gangsta Rap*. Next to it was a Reagan quote: *Out of these troubled times, our objective—a new world order—can emerge.*

Another item linked a Los Angeles physician, who had treated Eazy-E, comic Martin Lawrence, and funk star Rick James, to MK-ULTRA, a mind-control program developed by the CIA in the '50s. Eazy and James had supposedly been tools used to pollute young minds, while Lawrence's cross-dressing Big Momma films were attempts to undermine the masculinity of black males. (Tyler Perry received a mention too.)

Def Jam Records came in for particular scrutiny on the site, which argued that since its founding by the *powerful and mysterious "enlightened one"* Rick Rubin, the legendary label has been a hotbed of *satanic warfare against hip hop*. Videos by Jay-Z, Kanye, and Rihanna were cited for *patently satanic iconography that promoted teen suicide*. These artists were *controlled whether wittingly through the security of hell by satanic blood oath or unwittingly through MK-ULTRA programming.* Non–Def Jam performers cited for satanic influences were Lil Wayne and Chris Brown. Further down the home page D found more speculation:

The satanic gestures and ramblings of these artists is just the tip of an iceberg. Don't miss the forest for the trees. They are controlled. Keep the pressure and spotlight on them. Reeducate and reprogram them if necessary. But bring them back home from the clutches of NWO, a.k.a. New World Order.

D wasn't sure if he wanted to go forward. This comingling of hip hop, government mind control, and Satan unsettled him. He'd heard bits and pieces of all this paranoia in conversations on tour buses and in VIP booths. It was crazy stuff. Yet there was something strangely compelling about it. Plus, it's where the trail seemed to lead.

So D went to a message board and typed in:

I'm looking for a copy of a marketing report by a company called Sawyer on the hip hop audience circa late '80s. The late, great writer Dwayne Robinson worked on it and I'd like to see a copy. I'm willing to pay for the pleasure.

He included his e-mail address at the end of the message.

Not thirty seconds later his BlackBerry buzzed. The message was from TRUEGOD@hiphopcointelpro.com. He wanted to know: *Who the fuck are you?*

D hit him back with a little bio and mentioned his relationship to Dwayne Robinson. Two minutes passed before Truegod's next message: *Meet me at the corner of 116th and St. Nicholas tomorrow at 1 p.m.*

CHAPTER 8
THE MESSAGE

D stood at the corner of 116th Street and St. Nicholas, an intersection once notorious for drug trafficking. Back in the '70s, Nicky
Barnes's self-described "council" of heroin dealers made daily deliv-
eries of smack that had junkies lined up for "the package" like they
were waiting for theater tickets. During crack's vicious reign in the '80s
there were crack houses up and down 116th, where a generation of base
heads sucked away their futures.

So many rap records of the '80s and '90s were inspired by inter-
sections like this one. KRS-One, Biggie, Eazy-E, and countless others
translated the paranoia and pathos of the illegal street transactions into
verbal blaxploitation movies. It was on 116th Street that some of these
urban griots, these proud street reporters, turned drug dealing into
musical entertainment, taking their narratives into self-congratulatory
boasts that would have appalled Curtis Mayfield. But at least that first
wave of MCs were pioneers, experimenting with storytelling no one was
sure would work. Drug narratives went on to have the calculation of
market research and the freshness of soap opera drama. At least that's
how they sounded to D's ears.

The street entrepreneurs of old 116th Street had given way to real
estate developers, who were refurbishing buildings and constructing
mixed-use sites. Now you could live in your spanking-new condo and
go downstairs to score a latte. Businesspeople from Senegal, Ghana,

and throughout West Africa had reclaimed the aging storefronts from disrepair and turned 116th into a new-world African marketplace of import/export between Harlem and their homelands.

Remnants of old St. Nick and 116th Street were still visible—cluttered bodegas, church ladies walking toward Canaan Baptist, some hardcore addicts who hadn't gotten the memo on the mayor's gentrification program. But to D's eye, they seemed like ghostly echoes of an old, fading Harlem, one soon to be forever lost to the bulldozer of investment.

This was on his mind as he watched a man approach him. He assumed the dude was Truegod, though he didn't look much like a Five Percenter. His dreads were long and gray, more like the limbs of an aging beast that the healthy hair of a man in his thirties. His skin was shiny, usually a sign of good health, but he was also gaunt and rawboned. His eyes were owlish behind thin-frame glasses; his lips, surrounded by gray hair, were reddish-black and cracked like dry ice. The man wore a loose-fitting, multicolored African top, something probably purchased in the neighborhood, but worn at the edges like a damaged flag. His pants were formless and ill-fitting, but not nearly as tattered as his unlaced white Adidas shell-toe sneakers.

"You D Hunter?"

"Yes I am, Truegod."

"Well, you ain't the only Hunter on this corner."

"Is that so?"

"Yeah. I watched you for a good fifteen minutes before I came over. I checked you out."

"That's true. I saw you peeking from behind that SUV across the street."

"Oh, okay. But I can't be too careful. Once they know you know, they can make life difficult. They control so much."

D decided if Truegod said "they" again he was gonna leave. This was a long shot anyway. Now that he could see Truegod really was paranoid, D considered cutting his losses and heading back downtown.

"I'm hungry," Truegod said. "I know a great Ethiopian place right down the street."

D nodded and began following the oddly dressed man east on 116th.

Ethiopian food is eaten with the fingers, using a hunk of injera bread to scoop up a medley of foods. D watched the spectacle of Truegod eat and talk, the couscous often dribbling off his cracked lips back to the plate (and sometimes his lap or the floor) with disgusted fascination.

"Truegod, you a Five Percenter?"

"No, but I understand the impulse. The black man is a God here on earth. A chosen person."

"I recognize you, Truegod. You used to be a writer. Harry Allen, right?"

"Harry Tate, actually. People used to confuse me with him and that other writer Greg Tate too. It's why I use Truegod now, and I've made my own space. No one covers the undercurrents of what's happening in hip hop like I do. No one. That's why I know why your friend Dwayne Robinson said what he said."

"*It was all a dream.*"

"That's right."

"Does it have something to do with the Sawyer report?"

"Does a DJ need a turntable?"

"Okay."

"Okay nothing. You said something about a fee?"

D pulled $500 out of his wallet and placed it on the table.

"You know that ain't nearly enough. Not enough for what I know."

"I'm not sure you know a damn thing."

"People would kill for what I know. In fact, they killed Dwayne for it."

D reached across the table, took Truegod by the dashiki, and pulled the man's dreadlocked head toward his. "Don't fuck with my man's memory and don't try to play it like a poker chip. I won't kill you, but I will fuck you up so bad you'll wish I had." D let go of Truegod and watched couscous drop from the edges of his mouth.

"I've been threatened before," Truegod replied, shaky and defiant.

D pushed the $500 across the table. "But you don't look like you've ever been paid."

"I want $5,000."

"Motherfucker, you better tell me something before I go upside your head."

"Look," Truegod said, lowering his tone while he fingered the money, "I'm sorry I was a little, you know, disrespectful in talking about your friend. I see how upset you are. After all, you came in good faith."

"Okay, I lost my temper," D admitted. "I was there when he died and I'm still not over it. You feel me?"

"Absolutely. So let me give you the short version: the Sawyer memorandum was more than a marketing survey; it was a blueprint on how to control hip hop and, in the process, the future of black America."

"*The Plot Against Hip Hop* was the title of Dwayne's book."

"I know that. He e-mailed me quite a bit recently. We ran some theories back and forth. He never thought I was too extreme. Not like some people. Everybody perceived him as real mainstream . . . and me? I'm supposed to be out on the fringe. Underground and shit. But Dwayne knew firsthand how shit can get twisted up."

"Where's the memorandum?"

"You meet me in front of my apartment building in three hours with the rest of the money and I'll give you a copy and fill in some of the blanks."

"Five thousand isn't a lot of money if it's as important as you say."

"I've been offered more for it. I even got an offer once just to put it up on my website. But secrets only have power as secrets. I knew if I put it up on my site I'd just be another angry old-schooler with a beef." Truegod took a piece of paper out of his pocket and wrote out his address with a pencil.

"People would probably think I made the whole thing up. That it's a hoax or something. If Dwayne Robinson had used it in his book, people would have paid attention. They would have listened to him. I think that's why he's dead. Now, that $5,000 is no money to a lot of people, but it's a lot of money to me. It'll get me down to Costa Rica and a little place by the beach. I can still blog from there, you know. So meet me at my place and bring cash."

CHAPTER 9
BLACK STEEL IN THE HOUR OF CHAOS

Ddidn't come back to Harlem with $4,500 in cash. He brought $1,500 in cash—three five hundred–dollar bills. The rest was in a cashier's check made out to Harry Tate. Truegod clearly wasn't big on banking, so the check was intended more as bait than payment. Truegod, he thought, didn't figure to tell him everything he knew right away. D hoped the check would both distract and frustrate the writer into revealing more than he planned. If things went well they'd roll down to D's bank together to cash the check. If Truegod tried some sneaky shit D would just tear the check up and, maybe, stomp a hole in the dreadlocked man's chest.

While the block was dotted with signs of rehabilitation (scaffolding, dumpsters, lunching workmen), Truegod lived in a dingy tenement yet untouched by the forces of development. There were even two red-eyed, jail-looking dudes lounging outside—one shirtless with a white skullcap and sagging jeans, the other in a red T-shirt and matching red Yankee cap. D hated the liberties people took with tradition in the name of style even more than the reckless eyeballing this dynamic duo aimed his way. The kid repping the Bloods' colors raised a red flag, so to speak, but D felt confident he could subdue them efficiently if it came to that.

The rank aroma of mildew and garlic filled his nostrils in the building's small lobby. Next to the mailboxes and buzzer was a notice that the city was foreclosing on the property. It was only a matter of time before someone scooped the building up and made the place safe for white-collar folks looking to cut ninety minutes off their commute. For the moment the tenement was still home to working-class people like the nice Haitian woman and her heavyset daughter D encountered in the lobby; he helped navigate their shopping cart past the heavy metal front door. D then eschewed the elevator and took the gray marble staircase, which was dusty and had windows that looked out onto a narrow, sunless alley.

He had ventured up staircases like this a million times to visit friends, see women, and, for pay, instill fear and/or confidence in someone. A lot of these places tended to be shotgun buildings with rooms off a long central hallway. Some were so ancient that showers were in the kitchen and the toilet in some other room, the plumbing having been installed in the early twentieth century and then fitfully updated every other decade or so. D knew all that history would be cleaned up as soon as the building was finally purchased. They'd probably have Jacuzzis and shit.

Truegod would be long gone by then. So would the smell of pig's feet and vinegar that filled the air on the fourth floor. It was a lingering scent of Southern black life that reminded him of Sundays when his mother's cooking chased him out of the apartment in search of Mc-Donald's french fries.

When D knocked on the door, Truegod popped open three locks before cracking the door open. "Wasn't sure you were coming," he said.

"Well, I'm just full of surprises," D replied.

There had once been a great store called Rock and Soul Records on Seventh Avenue near Madison Square Garden that was always the best place to grab the hottest twelve-inch singles. Truegod's apartment was a reasonable facsimile. There were racks of vinyl against the walls. Posters and photos were taped and tacked up everyplace else. A recording of Mr. Magic's legendary radio show on WBAI was playing low on some unseen boom box. A banged-up Intel desktop sat on what would usually be called the living room table. Next to it was an old warhorse of an HP printer and clippings above it from periodicals as diverse as *Nylon*, the *Economist*, and *Vibe*.

"You got the money?" Truegod stood in the center of the room eyeing D nervously. D reassured him by pulling out a white Chase envelope and handing it over to the writer. Truegod immediately ripped it open and his face registered despair. "A check? I said cash only."

"Okay, we'll go to my bank and cash it. But we don't make another move until you hook me up."

"A check?" Truegod muttered again, and then disappeared into another room.

Under different circumstances D would have enjoyed rifling through Truegod's inviting collection of old-school vinyl. D noticed the Classical Two's *Rap's New Generation*, Teddy Riley's first credit as a full-blown producer, which made him half smile, but his face quickly reverted to stone when Truegod reappeared. There was a stack of papers in his right hand and a small-caliber revolver in his left. "They got Dwayne Robinson, but they ain't getting me. You hear me?"

"I won't let that happen, Truegod."

"But you were there when Dwayne died. Who's to know you didn't do the deed?" Truegod waved the gun threateningly in D's direction.

"Listen, motherfucker," D said, and took a step forward, "if I was gonna kill you I would have tossed you to the ground and stomped you the minute I came in the door. I'm not a killer and you know damn well you're not either, so put the jammy down and hand me those papers."

Truegod contemplated D's words and then tossed the pile of paper over to him. Roughly fifty pages were held together by a single brat clip squeezed into a hole in the upper left-hand corner. It looked like a third-generation copy and was printed on a kind of treated fax paper D vaguely remembered from his youth. The cover sheet read: *THE HIP HOP AUDIENCE: Its Attitudes, Trends, Demographics, and Future.* Below that was: *SAWYER MARKET GROUP, 1700 Broadway, New York City.* It was dated February 1989.

"I need to make a copy," D said.

"And I need that check cashed."

D nodded at the gun. "Let's go then."

Truegod slid the weapon between his belly and belt.

As they moved toward the door, D asked, "You do know how to use that?"

"Aim and pull the damn trigger. Stupider guys than me have shot people."

"And smarter guys than you have shot innocent people."

As they walked down the staircase Truegod made an important admission: "Yours wasn't the only e-mail I got recently about the memorandum. Lately I've been receiving more inquiries about that than where Tupac's living now. No one cared before Dwayne was assassinated."

"But you trusted me?"

"As much as I could anyone. I knew I needed to make a move. You seemed the least dangerous. You have a rep for being soft-hearted."

"Thanks. I try."

"But you see I still got my piece."

"Who contacted you?"

"Some people I've heard things about, you know. It made me look under my bed at night. I guess I could have made a deal with them, but then you got at me."

"So Dwayne's death and this pile of papers are somehow connected."

"Just like I believe Kanye West is a follower of Satan."

"As in the devil?"

"Believe me," Truegod said, "I've seen the psychiatric reports."

The two youngsters hanging outside the building were gone now. The workmen had finished lunch and were back grinding on the soon-to-be-revived buildings. A gypsy cab rolled past on its way toward St. Nick.

D clutched the report in the crook of his arm, like a Bible or a football. Truegod glanced nervously up and down the block. D could feel that the molecules on the street had shifted in the twenty minutes he'd been in Truegod's apartment. A gray cloud had appeared overhead. Rain was imminent. D took Truegod by the arm and they headed toward the waiting black sedan.

"It's not gonna take long to get that cash, is it? You know how things are. Cash is the only way to keep a secret. It's the only thing without a real computer trail now. I get your cash and I can make it to Costa Rica with only small blips on the screen. Little blips, you know. Nothing too traceable. Nothing worth remembering."

Truegod's rambling was irritating D and taking up a little too much of his attention. So D was a beat late in noticing the two youngsters from earlier come running out of an alleyway, their eyes John Blazed on herb, with box cutters poised to strike. D caught the bare-chested one with a side kick, buckling the fool's right knee and sending him screaming to the ground.

Unfortunately, the delay in D's awareness would prove fatal for Truegod. As the writer attempted to draw his gun, the red-garbed attacker slashed his face, his arm, and then his jugular in three rapid back-and-forth swings with his left hand. Truegod went down to his knees, clutching his throat, trying to hold back the blood as his life flowed away through his fingers.

D knew he had a problem. This wasn't just some kid with a blade. This guy was a trained killer. He turned toward D and chuckled, amused by the spasm of fear that crossed D's face. At first D was gonna go for the bare-chested dude's cutter, but they were too close to the second assassin. D dropped the Sawyer memorandum on the ground, freeing his right hand. The papers, not very well secured, scattered along the Harlem sidewalk. A few broke free, getting stuck in Truegod's blood.

As the kid moved toward him, D snatched the plastic lid from a garbage can and flung it hard with two hands into his face. The Blood raised his hands in defense and D threw himself into his attacker's mid-section, sending them both to the pavement with D's skull driving into the guy's sternum. When they landed, all the wind went out of his opponent and the box cutter fell to the ground. D rolled off him, landed on his knees, and then reared back to push a heavy right hand into the fool's face.

But that intention was never realized. Cause the next thing D knew everything had changed to his favorite color—black.

That night D had a dream.

He was standing in the middle of a two-lane highway surrounded by desert. He was wearing blue jeans and a torn sack of a canvas shirt. He was barefoot. His back was in pain, as if he'd been sliced in vertical lines by a long slender knife or whip. There was the metal taste of blood in his mouth.

Dwayne Robinson sat behind a desk on the side of the road with the glow from his laptop on his face, but this glow wasn't blue or white. It was reddish rose, the color of blood diluted with water. Dwayne was typing and oblivious to D's presence. A sheet of paper, pushed by a sudden gust of wind, brushed against D's leg and then fluttered away. Another sheet floated up. Then two, three, ten, twenty sheets came his way, bouncing over various parts of his body and down the empty two lanes.

D snatched one paper out of the air and tried to read the words, but it was nearly impossible. They were typed, tight together, single spaced, and fractured. *Andyoudon'tstopthebodyrockfeeltheheartbeat*. Hip hop phrases turned into unreadable gibberish.

A tour bus came down the road and deafening break beat accompanied it, something by Clyde Stubblefield chopped, sampled, and enhanced by the Bomb Squad. The bus stopped and revelers of all persuasions suddenly stood in front of him—their hands filled with popcorn, St. Ides malt liquor, Cîroc vodka, KFC, Pizza Hut, and Sprite.

At the end of the line of people there was a faceless, raceless man somehow guzzling Olde English 800 without a mouth. The can now empty, the faceless man looked up, as did his fellow travelers, at a noose hanging from a lamppost.

Then it was dark and the two-lane highway was now a country road and the moon hung low and the revelers held torches and wore white hoods, and Dwayne, still sitting by the roadside, kept on typing. A cheer went up and the faceless man held up D's penis for inspection and D looked down as he twisted in the heavy wind from the noose around his neck.

CHAPTER 10
THE BLUEPRINT FOR HIP HOP

You could never tell whether it was day or night in D Hunter's apartment. Heavy drapes covered the windows; the walls and ceiling were black, as was most of the furniture. On one wall was a framed photo of D and his relatives from back when he was the baby of the Hunter family. Next to it was a letter from his mother, written years ago, when the psychic wounds from the deaths of his three brothers were still painfully fresh.

D's apartment was a place of mourning, his own personal tomb of grief. It was twelve noon outside, but you'd never know it if you saw D curled up under black sheets, bandages on his head, hands, and shoulders, and a bottle of painkillers on the nightstand. So when he slowly awakened there was nothing that suggested day or night, the ambiguity that he craved, a sense of being lost in a dayless time. He'd always felt time was a trap. Everything that took place in the past was so present in his life, it was like tragic events kept happening over and over, even as new memories—many of them equally painful—rolled atop them, adding layer after layer, each darker than the one before.

This day, however, his physical pain was more pungent than any memory. The slashes on his body stung, particularly a nasty one on the fat part of his left hand. The back of his head throbbed where a baseball bat had introduced itself to the base of his skull. Pain pulsed through his head as D stirred, so he moved slowly, hoping it would delay the feeling he'd had his ass kicked.

Being HIV-positive always complicated his recovery from any altercation. How would his body respond? Would it weaken his already questionable immune system? Would it take him months to come back from something that, in his otherwise great condition, should take just weeks?

So far, so funky. Since returning home from the hospital D had laid up, hoping to get back out in the field by the weekend. He'd promised himself to chill out, especially after the shouting match he'd had with Fly Ty.

"Why is it that old hip hop writers die when you're around?" Ty had asked sarcastically.

"Because I'm apparently a bad bodyguard but a damn good detective."

Ty was actually very concerned about D and, also, quite embarrassed that a glorified security guard had apparently flushed out Dwayne's assassins. The MO had been the same as Dwayne's hit: two Bloods with box cutters, plus a third—who in D's case applied the game-winning blow with a baseball bat. D knew he was lucky to be alive. The third man, who a workman described as a light-skinned black man or Latino in a Phillies jersey and cap, could have just as easily cut his neck when he fell to the ground.

The facts of the attack were these: the getaway car, a blue Audi, had been abandoned in Washington Heights with bloodstains on the seats, along with red clothes and a old Westside Connection CD (which D couldn't believe anyone would still listen to, much less any self-respecting East Coast thug). The cops did their CSI thing to the car, comparing fibers, etc., from the Dwayne Robinson crime scene, but there were no matches. They did find hair in the Audi that belonged to a Caucasian, but since the car had been stolen from a white family in Hackensack, New Jersey, they weren't convinced it was significant. In short, no forensic evidence tied the two stabbings together beyond the choice of weapons and the presence of a third man with a car.

The gang squad found the evidence inconclusive. Gang initiation or paid hit? A paid hit over a decades-old marketing report? No, *two* paid hits over articles about hip hop. That didn't impress the NYPD. Fly Ty thought it was too much of a coincidence that D was involved in two initiation incidents so close together. But he too found the Sawyer memorandum theory "a silly load of bullshit." Hence the shouting match.

It didn't help that Fly Ty had answered, "It's in our system," when asked about the cassette found on Dwayne's body.

"Which means we'll hear it when?"

"It's an audio tape that is, as far as we know, tangentially, if at all, connected to an gang initiation."

"I thought murders in Soho were a priority for NYPD."

"They are. Except when it conflicts with matters of national security."

"What's a terror threat have to do with the cassette?"

"Don't act stupid, D. The team that handles audio recordings and such is backed up with intercepts of phone calls and tapes of meetings about possible terrorism in the city. It's a major investigation."

"And you know about it?"

"Yeah, they like to share here at NYPD. Anyway, you silly motherfucker, Dwayne's tape isn't on the back burner. It just isn't in the front. Our folks are excellent. As good as the FBI. But we only have so many ears."

D mulled all this over as he stood in boxer shorts in his small kitchen dropping strawberries, bananas, and whey protein into his blender. As he poured apple juice over this healthy concoction and turned on the blender, he wondered why that third attacker hadn't taken another whack at him. Prone and unconscious, D had been an easy target. Another hit and he wouldn't be making a fruit shake. No, he would be up in heaven joining his brothers in a two-on-two game like the ones back in the Tilden projects.

Maybe it was the workmen, one of whom came over with a hammer, or the approaching sirens of New York's Finest alerted by the call of one of Harlem's model citizens. When the police finally arrived there were just two men on the pavement, one dreadlocked and dead, the other bald and bleeding. And there were the papers. Tattered, dirty, ripped, and floating away in the breeze from a coming rainstorm.

After pouring his protein shake into a tall glass, laying out his regime of antiviral meds on his countertop, and digesting it all in one long gulp, D's mind refocused on the papers on the floor by his bed. Of the original fifty or so pages, D now had thirty-nine. He suspected that some had never been there in the first place, that whatever the late Mr. Tate had given him had been incomplete from the start. Maybe he'd been playing his own game and was holding back on D until the check was cashed. Others were undoubtedly destroyed or lost in the attack. Three of them were smeared with Truegod's blood.

So what D now possessed were like pieces of ancient parchment, links to some long-hidden wisdom. Or, at least, what passed for wisdom in 1989. Page 3 began:

Hip hop is an expression of black youth that was born out of the streets of the Bronx and Harlem in the early- to mid-'70s. It embraces a variety of disciplines that have proven to be attractive to young people in the U.S. as well as in Europe and Asia. It is a cul-

tural movement with social, commercial, and increasingly political applications. From a demographical viewpoint it is making inroads on the terrain once dominated by rock and roll and is growing as a determiner of cool with each passing year.

Page 7 said:

Though the DJs, breakdancers, and graffiti writers were the early heroes of the culture, the record industry's growing acceptance, and exploitation, of rap recordings has already made rappers the culture's commercial vanguard. Because the average rap record contains four to five times the lyrical content of an R&B song, the possibilities for sending commercial ("My Adidas"), political ("The Message"), and behavioral ("Criminal-Minded") messages go beyond any other pop artistic form of African-American expression. While young film-maker Spike Lee suggests new possibilities in that medium, the inexpensive nature of rap records and its grassroots distribution make it the truest voice of the young black mind.

Nothing earth-shattering. D looked deeper into the report and on page 25 found a section titled, *Recommendations.* That's where the fun began. "As the first fully formed community-inspired art movement since the cultural nationalists of the late '60s, hip hop has great potential for directing the energy and hopes of a generation. The danger here is that the growing presence of Nation of Islam and Five Percent Nation references, plus the gang affiliations of the emerging West Coast scene, could lead the culture in general, and young black America in particular, down the same ghettocentric path that created the U.S. organization and the SLA on the West Coast and Islamic-inspired thugs like

Philadelphia's Black Mafia. Right now these tendencies are balanced by the Afrocentric philosophy of Professor Molefi Asante of Temple University, the antiapartheid movement linked to Nelson Mandela, and the proto-hippie leanings of the Native Tongues (De La Soul, A Tribe Called Quest).

> *It is this report's contention that a targeted use of seed money (to buy or found labels, fund production companies), brand associations (connecting rap figures to significant brands via advertising and marketing), and strategic alliances (with filmmakers, entrepreneurs, "gangsters") could change hip hop's direction and, in a broader sense, that of black America. This opportunity, whether used for good or evil, is pregnant with opportunity for some entity with vision and financial resources to manifest them.*
>
> *Public Enemy's Chuck D said famously that his group's goal is to create several thousand black leaders. Hip hop, overall, has done that and more. The question, however, is where these leaders will take their constituents; to Dr. King's integrated promised land, to the Nation's angry separatism, to street hegemony, or to some destination unforeseen at this time.*

This was interesting stuff. And pretty prophetic, D thought. In a way, it had all happened. The boardrooms and ad campaigns of the early years of the twenty-first century both took hip hop as a given, its most potent figures embraced, at least in business, at the highest levels of corporate America. Fear of Islam was everywhere in white America, but Louis Farrakhan was dying as a revered figure among blacks and Muhammad was as common a name as Leroy or Washington had once been. The gangster ethos, of course, was omnipresent and had become a secular religion with rules of behavior as rigid as Vatican Bible study.

Implicitly laid out in this memorandum was the role of capital. The ability to fund hip hop would result in the ability to guide it. Some would even say control it. If that's what had happened we could all name the culprits—the decreasing universe of major labels, a few greedy taste-makers, and the base materialism that drove the American Dream.

Really good stuff for 1989, D thought, but who would kill over this? What self-respecting street thug would risk incarceration over this? Somebody must have paid them to kill. If there was a connection be-tween the papers in his hand and the murder of two old-school hip hop writers, the answer had to be found, as it was always and forever, in following the money.

At some point during this period, probably after *The Relentless Beat* was published, Dwayne had participated in the research and writing of the Sawyer memorandum, which could be seen as a market-focused version of his book. It was easy to see why they'd approach Dwayne—he was one of hip hop's first critic/journalists with any above-ground credibility and had proven himself capable of a book-length narrative.

Plus he was a true believer in the culture's ability to positively trans-form black America and, maybe, the world. And since cultural studies books, even classics, rarely paid serious money, he was likely eager to turn his insights into a real check.

While Dwayne would always be one of D's heroes, the compromise implicit in the writer's participation in the marketing survey was plain to see. As high-minded as Dwayne's writing about hip hop was, taking a job to help maximize its nonmusical sales potential was no different than the path so many MCs, breakdancers, and graffiti writers would take over the next decade in search of higher profits and a wider audi-ence. No wonder Dwayne never talked about the Sawyer memorandum.

It was a document of just the kind of commercial compromise *The Relentless Beat* was so judgmental about. Maybe by documenting (or creating?) a conspiracy against hip hop, Dwayne was trying to cleanse his own soul. To revisit your youth in middle age is to attempt to rewrite your history, D thought. Must have been a strange, sad journey back in time for him. Did Dwayne somehow blame himself for helping steer things in a direction that might have created a conspiracy where none existed?

But Dwayne was dead and Truegod was too. D had been laid up in bed with multiple stab wounds. History hadn't stabbed all three of them. Those knives had been as tangible as his tall chai latte, and way more lethal. D put the report down and was maybe a bit closer to understanding Dwayne, but still not sure why he was dead.

CHAPTER 11
SOUND OF THE POLICE

The light-skinned man had freckles and a receding hairline that could have been disguised by a baldie, but Peter Nash was way too vain to cut off any of his wavy black hair. He used his plastic knife and fork to saw through his extremely long Hampton Chutney dosa with gusto. "He got done right around the corner, huh?" he asked, already knowing the answer.

"Yeah," D replied, then took a sip of his hot chai. D didn't like Peter Nash very much, but the man knew a lot of things about the hip hop world and D hoped he'd pass on a useful detail or two.

"Looks like a gang initiation," D said, "but you don't think so."

"Do you? I deal in the tangible, D," Nash said, and took another bite. "You know that."

"Yeah, right," D mumbled in reply.

"Hey." Nash stopped sawing the dosa and looked D in the eye. "Detective Williams has watched out for me. And he's watched out for you, I'm told, though I have no idea why. Now, if you wanna ask me some questions, just know any answer I give is out of respect for him. And I enjoyed Mr. Robinson's books too. But if this was just about me and you, I'd be having my dosa by myself."

Swallowing his pride along with his chai, D said, "I understand. No disrespect intended." He sighed and nodded, thinking about how hard it was to deal with the hip hop cop.

Back in the early '90s, an enterprising New York City detective began connecting the dots between hip hop artists, their criminal associates, and ongoing investigations involving drug possession and trafficking, carrying unlicensed guns, and various assaults. The detective wasn't simpleminded about the rap/crime relationship. Just because they rapped about crime didn't make them criminals. What was interesting to the detective was the fact that so many MCs, by the nature of their upbringing and celebrity, were either targets of crime or employed ex-offenders.

Few other legal businesses in this country were as open to employing young black men with criminal records as hip hop. They worked as roadies, party promoters, bouncers, security, record producers, managers, and label heads.

There was no question that hip hop was a vehicle for so many young black folks to move away from a criminal lifestyle. But not all these men and women were able to cut their old ties so easily. In fact, some used hip hop not for transformation, but camouflage. The mobility of MCs and their entourages, especially on tour buses, allowed for the interstate transport of all kinds of lucrative merchandise (marijuana, cigarettes, automatic weapons), while others used this burgeoning business as a way to launder money. The question of how much the MCs knew about these activities, and whether they profited from them, varied from performer to performer. Obviously, the bigger the star, the more likely they jettisoned their hoodiest friends and separated themselves from any possible criminality. But if you were a youngster on the way up or a vet on the decline, well, you might get down.

But the truth was that creating rap records didn't automatically make you a tough guy. Many MCs were moving targets, prey for stick-up kids and extortionists. It wasn't unusual for an MC to be robbed of jewelry and cash at a nightclub, or to have their home burglarized when they were on tour.

The complex web of affiliations and transactions was catnip to a smart cop. Knowing this world could lead to high-profile collars and promotions. So the NYPD detective developed a dossier on New York's most important hip hop figures, complete with arrest records, various places of business and residence, car registrations and license plate numbers, known associates with criminal records and label affiliations.

This dossier was one-stop shopping for NYPD whenever an MC had a run-in with the law (which happened often). By the time that original detective retired, the dossier had taken on a life of its own. It was passed along and other detectives took on the mantle of hip hop cop. Back when Jay-Z was still Bed-Stuy do-or-die rugged, and was accused in December 1999 of stabbing a dude for bootlegging his records, there was a hip hop cop on the scene. When Sean Combs, Jennifer Lopez, and Shyne were implicated in a nightclub shooting in that same fateful month, a hip hop cop interrogated the suspects (and helped build the case against Shyne). When Jam Master Jay was murdered in 2002, there was a hip hop cop outside the funeral taking down license plate numbers.

Police departments in Miami and Atlanta, cities that both attracted New York MCs and had their own dynamic local scenes, consulted with the Big Apple's hip hop cops and developed their databases. And databases is what they were. From binders and paper, the NYPD dossier evolved into an ever-growing digital guide to the places where street culture and street crime shook hands. For many, the existence of such intelligence gathering was *the* plot against hip hop. It was racial profiling at its most blatant and generated many an outraged article in the hip hop press.

Fly Ty suggested that D reach out to the latest incarnation of NYPD's hip hop cop, and D did it reluctantly. Nash was based out of a Midtown Manhattan precinct and had inherited the job of updating the database, so he kept himself abreast of any and all hip hop–related developments—from who hung out at Jay-Z's 40/40 Club to who visited Lil Wayne during his stay at Rikers Island on a gun possession charge.

Back around 2000 Nash had been doing a lot of work as a bouncer and approached D about work, but had gotten the brush-off because D had never quite trusted the guy. Because of the murder of his brothers and the resulting relationship with Fly Ty, D had spent a lot of time around cops and had developed his "Letter C" theory of policemen. Some were like calluses in that they'd built numbing scabs on their souls to protect them from feeling too much; some had become cynics, men and women who saw the dark side of every human interaction; some were just so cautious that they moved through the city desperate not to do anything dramatic as they glided quietly toward their pension; the crazy ones reveled in sticking their noses in every dirty gutter of the city; the courageous ones were a strong minority who managed to stay straight and righteous, no matter how deeply the job made them bend.

A great policeman, like his main man Fly Ty, managed to balance all these C words, manifesting the best aspects of each of the qualities as he moved through the city's many worlds. Too much of any single C word and a policeman got as warped as the values of the criminals pursued. In D's opinion, Nash was as curved as the edges of a college sophomore's Frisbee. Way too calloused, cynical, and corrupt to be protecting anything but his own self-interest.

D couldn't deny that Nash was a survivor. He was in his early forties, on the force nearly twenty years, and headed toward some lucrative gig doing corporate security if he kept his nose clean for another year or so.

"So," Nash said with a smile, "a conspiracy? You talking about the Illuminati. That's everybody's favorite hip hop conspiracy theory."

"You don't think there's anything to it, do you?"

"Ignorant folks love the idea that an all-seeing, all-knowing cabal of motherfuckers gathered for annual meetings to move them around like chess pieces. They love it. Gives them a good damn excuse for the shit storm that's their life. Besides, how's a bunch of seventeenth-century motherfuckers gonna organize a bunch of twenty-first century niggas to do anything? Can you see a man in a white wig convincing Jay-Z to dump Dame Dash?"

They both shared a laugh at that.

"You can only prove and disprove *theories* until you get ahold of those two kids who stabbed your friend. That's hard enough—red bandannas, white T-shirts, baggy jeans, colorful sneakers. That'll get you a nice long list of suspects."

"I hear you. But will you at least keep your eye out for connections? Dwayne's book was definitely about hip hop. It definitely had something to do with revealing old secrets. Maybe secrets someone in hip hop might not want out. It's right up your alley."

"D, I do a lot of things. I don't have much time for pro-bono side projects."

"Listen, all I want you to do is to ask some people questions about what Dwayne might have talked to them about. That's all."

"Okay," he said quietly. "I'll think about it. Thanks for the dosa."

After Nash left, D wondered if the meeting had been a good idea. Maybe the hip hop cop was Illuminati himself.

CHAPTER 12
CRIMINAL MINDED

D rarely ventured to the Boogie Down these days. He'd catch a Yankee game once or twice a year, but that was basically it. The Bronx, ground zero for one of the biggest global cultural movements of the late twentieth century, was essentially a nonfactor in the making and selling of hip hop in the twenty-first century. There were no major venues there; none of its natives, except Fat Joe, had any serious place on the charts.

Nowadays the Bronx was an old-school preserve where the hip hop past was honored, celebrated, and, to some degree, embalmed, its mummified remains a symbol of another city, revered and vilified and now long dead. Under Mayor Bloomberg there had been much-needed economic development and a huge upswing in affordable housing. The big empty, abandoned blocks of the '70s that were once a symbol of the city's defeat had been filled in by dedicated residents and smart city planners. The South Bronx was no longer Fort Apache and the Bronx was no longer burning, but the spirit of street-corner innovation that was the borough's legacy was no longer its heartbeat.

D was mulling this over as he sat in the lobby of the Bronx Saint's Nursing Home, a well-maintained institution in the borough's upscale Riverdale neighborhood. He was gazing up at a wall of framed pictures of BX landmarks—the Grand Concourse, the county courthouse, the original Yankee Stadium—as he waited to speak with a record business legend. A middle-aged Latino nurse, round and dressed in a nonde-script cream-colored uniform, came out and led him down a long hall-way and then out into a large, lovely garden overlooking the Hudson River. Sunning himself there in a wheelchair was a man in his late sev-enties who D had known for a couple of decades, and who'd also been a fixture in the R&B world decades before D was born.

Edgecombe Lenox sat with the sun shining on his full head of gray hair, Ray-Ban shades protecting his light brown eyes, a *North Carolina* powder-blue and white knit sweater, and matching slacks and leather slippers, with thin light blue socks. There was a diamond in one earlobe and a glittering blue-face Rolex on his right wrist. Though his tall, lanky frame was stuck in a wheelchair following two strokes, Edge (as he pre-ferred to be called) still had plenty of style.

"Youngblood," he said as D approached, "how's it hangin'?"

"Low," D replied, and then added, "but not as low as yours."

"Never that," Edge said with a laugh, and leaned up to receive D's hug.

D had met Edge through Dwayne Robinson years ago, when he was first setting up D Security and looking for contacts. Edge, who back then was a vice president for urban promotion at Universal Records, had hooked him up with a security gig for a record release party and they'd soon established a solid business relationship/friendship.

Edge had been a key inspiration/subject/source for *The Relentless Beat*, because the man's career pretty much spanned post–World War II music history. He'd been a sand dancer outside juke joints in his native Macon, Georgia, recorded doo-wop songs with buddies in Harlem after he'd escaped the Jim Crow South, rocked microphones from Virginia to Boston during the soulful '60s, and became a talent manager/label owner before being recruited as an executive for black/urban music when major corporations made their move into the scene in the '70s.

For the next twenty years or so Edge played ring-around-the-record-labels, moving from Capitol to Epic to RCA to MCA, until he finally ran out of jobs as hip hop altered the landscape in the '90s.

Unlike most R&B–bred heads, Edge wasn't immediately disdainful of this new movement. Having lived through jump blues, cool jazz, rock and roll, R&B, rock, soul, free jazz, funk, and disco, he wasn't intimidated by change. "Our music changes because our people are chameleons," Edge told D several years back. "We change our slang. We change our threads. We change what we think is cool and what we think is corny. And all that ends up in our dance, and our dance responds to our music."

If Dwayne had been D's adopted older brother, Edge had been his kinda grandfather, and the two men shared the same feeling of loss. So D told him everything he knew, from the tape to Truegod to the Bloods.

"I remember Jimmy Sawyer," Edge said thoughtfully. "He ran that marketing company."

"Can I talk to him?"

"Oh, he's long dead. Too much coke, too little sleep. Bane of that '80s generation. Me? I did a line or two but I stuck with weed and bourbon. It's why I'm still here."

"What about D talking about a 'remix' and Truegod talking about a government conspiracy?"

"Well, a dying man could be talking about anything. I don't put a lot of stock in that. It's the *Citizen Kane* theory of life."

"What's that?"

"It's a movie. At the beginning of the movie Kane dies and says a word—something about roses. They spend the whole movie trying to figure out what the words mean. Every damn body ever since is always trying to figure out what a dying man's last words mean. But me, I've seen several men die and not once did their last words make a damn bit of sense."

D sat there next to the old man feeling silly, until Edge cleared his throat.

"But let me say this: you can never go wrong suspecting that the government is involved in some plot to mess over black people. There's a long history, you know."

"I've read some stuff online," D responded, "but a lot of it sounds crazy."

"Well, I don't know what you read but this stuff is real, youngblood. You know about the Tuskegee experiment? They even made a movie of it."

"Some medical shit, right?"

"For years they shot up a gang of brothers with gonorrhea and syphilis to see what the fuck would happen. Like that was gonna be some surprise. And the U.S. government paid for the whole damn thing."

"That's foul."

"You know the government put mikes under Dr. King's bed. Hoover listened to that shit for fun," Edge explained.

"He got off listening to Dr. King sleeping?"

"Damn, you kids don't know shit about your history. King had a lot of female admirers and things happened."

"You telling me that Dr. King was crushing some groupies and the FBI was listening in? That's scandalous shit."

"He was a man just like you and me. When they make heroes out of plywood, not flesh, these things won't happen. But King made human mistakes; the government was all about harming a black leader. You know what COINTELPRO was?"

"I do. But that was way back in the '60s."

"The government has set up stings on black politicians—congressmen and mayors and activists of all kinds—in just the last few years."

"Didn't they catch some fool with bricks of cash in his refrigerator? Some politician from Louisiana?"

"Well, you do read more than the *Source*. He was set up by your tax dollars."

"So an anti–hip hop conspiracy is not impossible?"

"Possible. It's definitely possible. Get ten black people in a room talking about anything that might get them power or influence, I guarantee you one's a government agent and two want to be."

"Didn't know you were so political, Edge."

"I ain't political. I'm alive. Ain't a black person who's lived as long as I have who doesn't know that every federal agency with three letters—FBI, CIA, DEA, and especially that fucking IRS—will pull you down faster than a weedwhacker. Believe that."

"D's book was called *The Plot Against Hip Hop*. But the plot had to have failed. I mean, I don't like most of what passes for the music now, but there are so many hip hop–made millionaires. The culture sells everything under the sun and is all over the world. It feels like a success to me."

"But the thing is, do all these rich black folks really own hip hop?"

"They own themselves. A guy like Jay-Z, for example, owns his brand and does with it what he pleases."

"Maybe Jay-Z has reached some kinda nirvana, maybe he's become the guru of grandiosity he always said he was, but it don't feel to me that we—meaning black folk—actually control something we built from the ground up. You know, D, that was the big dream back in the '60s and '70s. Black music was like oil to Arabs—it was gonna be our way to build a larger economic machine. Empower people through our culture."

"Yeah, that's one of the things Dwayne Robinson talked about in *The Relentless Beat*."

"He did indeed."

"Was it a conspiracy that this didn't happen?"

"Black folks just wanted a corporate gig—an Am Ex card, expense account, and an office in a Sixth Avenue skyscraper were enough to satisfy most of them. I know cause I was one of them. It don't take a conspiracy to drown a thirsty man. Just give him an overflowing cup of water."

The two men sat quiet for a minute, as Edge seemed lost in his memories. D wondered whether it was time to leave.

"Yo," Edge said finally, "they had a report back then too."

"About what?"

"It was known as the Harvard Report. It was commissioned by CBS Records to study how the corporate labels could take over black music from the Motowns, Stax, and other black music labels. And they actually did what was in that report, so this kinda research is nothing new. They dissect it like a frog in biology class. They see how our heart works and what pumps blood to our brain and then pull us apart for sport. That's how they did us then and that's how they do us now, and I guess they will continue until we can finally make them stop. Dwayne knew that. In fact, he understood it better than I do. He was really good at looking under the chassis of the car and comprehending how the gears worked."

"Do you think that's why he died?"

"Youngblood, I'm sitting up in a old-folks home in the damn Bronx. So what's happening in the streets today I won't pretend to know. But this I do know: the world of black success is always a lot smaller than it seems from the outside. You go to any town, from New York to Lake Charles, Louisiana, to Akron, Ohio, and you go to any club that's frequented by our people, and you'll see the black undertaker, the black banker, and the black minister (or his children) up in that piece, alongside the people just coming through the town—the athletes, the entertainers, the dancers, and the actors.

"What I'm saying, youngblood, is that everyone knows each other and everyone's connected, from the highest of the high to the lowest of the low. I bet you that you are just one or two conversations away from knowing what you want to know. You just haven't been to the right party on the right night yet. It could be tomorrow in New York or it could be six months from now in LA. So for Dwayne, and for me, please keep asking."

"Of course." D reached inside his black suit and pulled out a plastic vacuum pack containing two Cohibas, top-notch Cuban cigars.

"Youngblood, you are my main man."

"What does your doctor say about these?" D asked as his friend slipped the cigars into his pocket.

Edge chuckled. "The average life expectancy for a black man of my generation is something like sixty-four. You know, like that Chris Rock joke—between hypertension, cancer, and the KKK, I should have been dead years ago. So a Cuban cigar at this point can only knock a day off, or maybe two, cause I've already used up most of my years."

"Right. Edge, you are gonna outlive me."

"Well, I outlived Dwayne."

"Yeah."

"Sad. A night-owl degenerate such as myself is still sucking God's good air and a homebody writer gets stabbed to death over some street shit."

"Yeah."

"You taking your meds?"

"Absolutely."

"Good. Don't make me any sadder, D."

"No way I would, Edge."

D got up and headed out of the nursing home, his head buzzing from his talk with Edge and anxious to get back to Manhattan.

CHAPTER 13
PARTY FOR THE RIGHT TO FIGHT

The Macy's event went off smoothly. The crowd was mostly black and Latino teens who, despite some trepidation on the part of management, had been well behaved. The problem was, there weren't very many of them. Gibbs made a cameo appearance. He smiled, shook D's hand warmly, and spent most of his time conversing with his corporate clients (a.k.a. ass-kissing). D listened in from the periphery as there was a lot of talk about whether this sparse turnout was a reflection of the "soft" market for rap records over the last few years. Sales had been sagging and hip hop radio was getting its butt kicked in most major markets by pop and Latin-oriented stations. The clients were wondering whether hip hop was losing its hold on America's youth. Gibbs was doing his best to put the best face on the marketing disaster.

But Gibbs's angst wasn't really D's concern. For him the light turnout just meant a nice comfortable day for D Security. Once the event was officially over, he headed up to the first-floor men's department and picked up a few items—two turtlenecks, three pairs of socks, and two slacks—all in shades of black. To D, charcoal, ink, midnight, and ebony were as vibrant as crimson, scarlet, rose, or anything else red had to offer. Satisfied with his purchase, D walked downtown on Seventh Avenue toward his apartment. It had been two weeks since Truegod's death and a month since Dwayne Robinson's, and there had been zero movement in either case.

After his recovery from the Harlem attack D had refocused on his business and lined up some choice gigs for D Security. They would handle security for the Rush Art for Life benefit in East Hampton, a Sprite commercial shoot in Los Angeles, and the BET Awards later in the year. The next afternoon some of his team were accompanying Kanye West to debut his first video game called *Graduate Student* at Best Buy on Broadway. His company's reputation as being dependable and effective had spread across the country, something D was incredibly proud of. If he could just focus on that fact, he'd have been quite content.

Still, Dwayne's murder nagged at him. He knew the death of a black man at the hands of other black men was never a priority for American justice. The new century hadn't changed that. None of the triggermen who'd put caps in his older brothers had done a day of time. Even D, who'd been so filled with righteous anger when Dwayne's blood was spilled on his clothes, had let things slide. Despite his initial outrage, D knew people got killed all the time in this country. It was a sea of violence that sometimes ebbed but never stopped flowing.

D's place was on Seventh Avenue in the 20s in the kind of high-rise condo that he'd actually come to despise. It was one of the many pieces of evidence that Bloomberg wanted condos as far as his eye could see. They were all over the city now (in the 20s on Sixth Avenue, from Chelsea up to the 40s, along Flatbush Avenue in Brooklyn). All of them uniform, disconnected from street life, and destroyers of the very flavor people came to the Apple for. It was a rich man's version of urban living, like something out of that *Fountainhead* book D had plowed through one semester to pass English lit.

Living in just the kind of monstrosity he disliked made his loathing of it deeper. He'd lived in a three-story, well-maintained Midtown tenement for over a decade, content to coexist with the sometimes dicey plumbing in exchange for being low to the ground and knowing all his neighbors. After a lengthy battle with developers and the city, the building was condemned and D, wanting to stay in the middle of town, found himself living in this new condo. He'd found that compromise was essential to survive in this new century.

As D hung and folded his new clothes, he listened to Public Enemy's first album, *Yo! Bum Rush the Show*, the one that had been so overshadowed by *It Takes a Nation of Millions* and their subsequent albums. D always had a soft spot for it, cause it reminded him that every adult is first a baby—promising, immature, inventive, and inexperienced. Sometimes there's more inspiration in the awkward first steps than in the confident classic, D thought. He saw himself in the sounds of PE's struggle to define their voice. D just hoped he was turning out as well as they had.

While Chuck and Flav rhymed on the title track of the album, D laid out his afternoon regimen of antiviral pills and gulped them down with a big swig of Evian. He sat listening, amused that stopping the bum-rushing of shows was just how he made his money.

He pulled out the Sawyer memorandum and was leafing through it, looking for a fresh angle on this old document, when his BlackBerry ring tone came on, Ice Cube's "The Wrong Nigga to Fuck Wit." It was Todd Smith, one of his staffers, calling to say Kanye's people were beefing about his absence. "You know how that camp is, D," Todd said. "I know you wanted a night off but they feel slighted. The video game people joined in too, so I think you should run through."

"All right," D answered, "I'll be over in thirty."

Reluctantly, D set down the report and headed to the shower. Afterward he put on his new selection of clothes and hailed a taxi down to Broadway between Houston and Bleecker, just a block from his office.

Metal barricades had been set up and male gamers, spiced with young female Kanye fans, were already standing in line. There was an NYPD cruiser outside, some skinny Best Buy staffers in T-shirts, and several of his well-dressed D Security folks. His peeps were supervising and manning key checkpoints. D had gone through all the details in the morning before heading up to Macy's and knew his crew had everything under control. But the client is always right, especially when every company out there wanted video game biz.

Kanye was at least two hours away, so D was wondering how to kill the time. Another walk-through of the store? Maybe a quick run to the office to check the mail? He was mulling his options when a black man in a thin, well-tailored beige suit and one of those mohawks where the hair peaks like a hill in the middle, approached him. The guy was around forty, with a thin mustache and the confident demeanor of someone who shopped via the *Robb Report*.

He reached his hand out to D and said, "You don't remember me, do you? I'm James Woodson. You guys on tour used to call me Woody. I met you when I was a tour manager for LL and you were doing security. Back then I wore Fila tracksuits and Air Force 1's exclusively."

"Okay, I remember you." Glancing at Woodson's wardrobe, D added, "Things have changed."

"And for the better."

"You think so?"

"Come on, man. Back then we were both scrambling to make it. Now we're businessmen. You own your company. I'm an executive at a video game company and we are killing it, dude."

For a few moments they reminisced about working with LL, a couple of crazy tours, and some of the other folks from those tours who they hadn't thought about in years. While D was a little nostalgic, Woodson seemed to look back at everything as a stepping stone to what he was into now.

"Best thing that happened to me back then was befriending these two guys who were putting together tour sponsorships for artists. Once the tour was over I ended up getting a marketing job with their company, Sawyer. I stayed there for a year and then got headhunted by these video game dudes and it's been sweet ever since."

"Sawyer, huh? Walter Gibbs did some time there too, didn't he? Just saw him today at an event my company handled down at Macy's."

Woodson shook his head in admiration. "Yeah, Gibbs. Wow. That dude learned quite a bit at Sawyer. I like my career a lot, but that man has done better than all of us. He got out of hip hop before the market changed."

"You ever hear of a marketing survey Gibbs and a writer named Dwayne Robinson worked on for Sawyer? It was a plan for the best ways to exploit the hip hop audience. People called it the Sawyer memorandum."

Woodson's face scrunched up, as if D had just passed gas. "When I was there we did three or four reports like that. JVC commissioned one. Nike had us do one. Some beer company—maybe St. Ides. Remember how foul that shit tasted?"

"Yeah, it was nasty. Probably the worst malt liquor ever."

"And that's saying a lot."

"No doubt. No doubt. So you guys did several reports, but I believe this one was different."

"How so?"

"Dwayne Robinson. The writer I mentioned."

"Yes. Robinson. I remember reading his shit. He never really understood what rap was about, did he?"

"What makes you say that?"

"It was about paper from day one. All that sociopolitical shit was accidental, or maybe incidental. You feel me? Just like this video game world. It takes a lot of technology to make this stuff. But essentially it's just a toy. Something to pass the time between living and dying."

"That's it?"

"That's it."

"Well, Dwayne felt the music was about more than that and he might have even thought the particular Sawyer memorandum I'm talking about was some plan—not just to sell music to the audience, but to manipulate the audience and the artist."

Woodson burst out laughing. "This Dwayne dude says all that with a straight face? This ain't the '80s. There's no antinigga machine—with all due respect to Chuck D, there's no plot to kill us. Bad shit happens to stupid people. Always has. Always will."

Both men turned toward a sudden flash of light, followed by the trill of excited girls and the bustle of those who genuflected to celebrity for a living. Kanye was in the building, resplendent in odd Japanese shades and some eclectic ensemble of BAPE and Gucci, with retro British Walkers on his feet. For D this distraction was well timed. Woodson had just insulted his dead friend and made a lot of what he believed in sound silly. Time to end this convo. Don't even get into the fact that Dwayne was dead. No need to even go there.

Woodson looked at Kanye and then asked, off-handedly, "You have a copy of the Sawyer memorandum you mentioned?"

The question surprised D. He shifted his gaze from the rap superstar back to the video game executive, who seemed different now. A bit lean and hungry. A touch anxious around the eyes. It was a look D had seen many times before at clubs just before someone got sucker punched.

"Yeah, I do," he said casually.

"Tell you what . . ." Woodson reached into his pocket and pulled out his card. "I gotta go talk to Kanye and his people, but send me a copy, okay. I'm sure I'll get some laughs out of it, like reading ancient hieroglyphics." He pushed the card into D's palm. "Get at me about that and I'll send a messenger over for it. You stay up now, dude."

"You do the same."

And then Woodson was down the steps and into the crowd of self-important souls who surrounded the MC. D watched as his peeps manned their positions, visible but unobtrusive, just as he preached at D Security meetings. He peered once again at Woodson, smiling, shaking hands, whispering to someone, and didn't know what to think. The man was welcome to his opinions about Dwayne, hip hop, and every other damn thing. He didn't dislike Woodson. He recalled him as a decent guy back in the day. One night in Denver, D had even played wingman for him, helping keep company with an obnoxious sista while Woodson wooed her better-looking friend.

Still, he wondered, why would the man want a copy of something he'd just sneered at? As D watched Kanye getting settled in on a make-shift dais, a video game console behind him and a dozen Sharpies laid out before him, he decided that he wasn't gonna give Woodson shit.

CHAPTER 14
MADE YOU LOOK

D hated interview rooms at police stations. He could feel the fear and manipulation of scores of investigations, like they were seeping from the walls. Still, he was happy to be there. He'd thought Fly Ty had forgotten him, but then the dapper DT had always been there for him.

It was a good recording, except for the fact that the radio was on, playing Nas's "Made You Look," and cars were honking like crazy.

"It sounds like they had this conversation by a tunnel at rush hour," Fly Ty said quietly.

D nodded, but said nothing. He was straining to hear the conversation. He didn't recognize the man speaking, which pissed him off since he very much wanted to.

"You want me to help you do some kind of book, huh?"

"Yes. That's what I do: write books." It was Dwayne Robinson, sounding like he was close to begging.

"That would be dangerous."

"I have the report," Dwayne said. *"I can use that. I don't need your permission. I'm asking for your cooperation. You could help me expose the whole thing."*

"I understand what you wanna do and why. I actually have no problem with it. But my coworker—I don't think he'll understand."

"Why aren't you afraid?"

The other man chuckled. *"We're all afraid of something."* Said like a sage. *"I'm just not afraid of this."*

"Okay. I'll take you at your word. But your coworker feels different?"

"Yes, he does. Me? I tried to remix things but you can only do that so much."

"What's that mean?"

"As truthful as I can be, Dwayne. There's no real value in exposing our activities. Only the truly determined conspiracy theorists are gonna pay attention. All these young people who buy today's music and the concert tickets and the cologne—they are not gonna care. They got a million Southern rappers to hear and two million Southern dances to learn. The only thing you should be paying attention to is staying safe."

"You threatening me, Malik?"

"No. I wouldn't touch you. I respect you a great deal, Dwayne. I mean that. But I can't protect you. You continue on this path and there could be consequences. Maybe you should call that bodyguard friend of yours, E."

"D? D Hunter?"

"Yeah, make a deal with him for security. It could be money well spent."

"So your not gonna help me?"

"No, but I'm not gonna stop you."

A car door opened, the noise of the big city filled the audio track, and then Dwayne could be heard saying, *"Shit."* And the tape ended.

"So," Fly Ty said, "that was Dwayne Robinson?"

"Absolutely."

"Robinson called the other man Malik. That name ring a bell?"

"I know some Maliks but they are young guys. This guy sounded at least forty. And you know something else? He sounded like a cop to me."

"Okay, Mr. Holmes," Fly Ty said. "How'd you deduce that?"

"Well, maybe not a cop, but some kind of government worker. There was something sneaky and bureaucratic in his voice. Am I wrong?"

Fly Ty clicked the eject button on the cassette player and slipped the tape into a plastic bag. "I've been in law enforcement nearly twenty-five years, D, and 'sounds like a cop' does mean something to me. But I couldn't cosign that in this case. On the other hand, the name Malik—that's actually useful. I'll call Robinson's wife and ask her if they have any friends with that name."

"I bet that's why his office was ransacked. Malik was there looking for any references to himself. Looking for the manuscript."

Fly Ty sighed. "All this tells us is that a man named Malik was involved in some project that Robinson was investigating about a book that had something to do with hip hop. We also know he wasn't gonna cooperate with Robinson in his research and that he knew someone who'd feel threatened by what Robinson was writing. That's all helpful."

"What's also helpful is that the person who was threatened probably wasn't two teenage Bloods. That was a hit, Fly Ty."

"Okay, Mr. Detective. You are making a leap. Maybe it's a smart one, but we are a long way from having any evidence linking those two killers to anything else."

"What about Truegod's death?"

"Lots of loose links. But NYPD isn't in the business of saving hip hop. If you can find some more substantial link between these two deaths other than an obscure marketing plan, we'll dig deeper."

"I'ma hold you to that, Fly Ty."

D caught a bus on Fifth Avenue; as it rolled downtown, he sat there thinking about money, secrets, and hip hop. The first two were the chief reasons many people were killed. Hip hop now seemed to be reason number three.

So who made money off the Sawyer memorandum? Who would benefit from hip hop becoming a highly marketable commodity and sapped of any political edge? A taxi paused next to the bus with an ad for Cîroc vodka on top; Diddy posed suavely next to a bottle. That was gonna be the problem trying to solve Dwayne's death. So many different kinds of people were getting paid off hip hop in so many different ways that it made the whole industry suspect. D needed to put himself back in the late '80s/early '90s and see what people and corporations had benefitted during that transitional period.

What the hell could they have done that justified two murders twenty years after the fact? The memorandum was a starting point and Diddy's alcohol ad was one possible end. What was the through line in the history of hip hop that results in Dwayne Robinson being stabbed dead on Crosby Street in Soho?

CHAPTER 15
ANTE UP

Brownsville was still awash in blood. Despite New York City's all-time low murder rate and crime figures that made the metropolis one of the safest big cities in America, in good old Brownsville—a Brooklyn neighborhood of endless public housing tracts, generations of poverty, and restless, hungry youth—folks were still getting killed regularly for stupid shit.

On the walls of apartment buildings, elevated subway stations, and malt liquor billboards, the C and B of Crips and Bloods were ubiquitous. Pint-sized gangbangers, strapped, insecure, and terribly thin-skinned, perpetuated self-genocide with a ruthlessness too reminiscent of Rwanda. Though they shared the names of infamous South Central gangstas, the menace involved wasn't drive-bys or the economic imperatives of crack-era cartels.

In twenty-first century Brownsville, the landscape was littered with minigangs—cousins, project floor neighbors, homies who met in juvie—who were organized around low-level drug deals, extortion, and assault. Some were as young as ten and had the nasty intelligence of the kids from Brazil's *City of God*, with whom they shared dismal prospects and the same desire for validation.

Ever since the days of Murder Incorporated, when tough Depression-era Jews from Brownsville carried out hits for the Mob, the neighborhood had spawned more than its share of hard-eyed, violent men. It's one reason Brownsville had a long tradition of adroit, dynamic fighters, with Mike Tyson both the most well known and notorious. Sometimes, walking down Livonia or Rockaway avenues, it felt as if the threat of violence was seeping up out of the ground, like the vapors from an over-run sewer, infecting the populace.

It was this legacy that D Hunter was part of, and it hurt to know that deaths—Brownsville deaths—had molded him as much as his mother's love or the books he'd read or the places he'd traveled to. Wherever D went, Brownsville was there with him, and unlike the BK MCs he sometimes protected, he knew this wasn't a good thing.

When D was growing up in the Ville, his subway stop had been Rockaway Avenue, right on the corner where Livonia intersected with the Samuel J. Tilden housing projects. Saratoga Avenue was the stop before Rockaway, and D had rarely gotten off there unless he was stopping by Betsy Head Playground, a New Deal–era athletic field and pool.

In the two decades since D had escaped the Ville, the city government, in its infinite wisdom, had constructed the Marcus Garvey Houses between Betsy Head and Tilden. Named after the visionary "Back to Africa" leader of the 1920s, the low-rise public housing complex had not exactly become a source of pride for the people of the diaspora. Garvey's construction had coincided with the crack era and so the buildings had been overrun by the epidemic, turning Brownsville an even grimmer shade of crimson.

In the '90s people would have laughed if you said there were Bloods in Brooklyn. But around the turn of the century, black inmates in New York City correctional facilities, tired of getting their asses kicked by the well-organized Latin Kings, used the Bloods brand to organize themselves under a banner. Supposedly, two OGs in Rikers were the key men behind this move, and as D sat on the Saratoga platform, he prepared to meet one of them. He'd gotten Ray Ray's call that afternoon.

"I'm about to earn that money, D."

"Go."

"I need you to come out to Brownsville tonight. I have a Blood I want you to meet."

"How much?"

"Just bring two Gs for him. But don't bring mine. Don't bring my cash out to Brownsville."

"I hear that. You sure this is serious?"

"This man is a real OG. Plus, he knows you from the Tilden projects, so it's all good. Meet me at the Saratoga Avenue IRT station at seven."

"Cool, I know it well."

Ray Ray came up the steps at seven-twenty p.m., fifteen minutes later than he'd suggested, but by ghetto standards about a half hour early. "What's good?"

"I dunno," D replied. "Anytime I have to do business in Brownsville, it's never a good thing. Is he meeting us up here?"

"I told you we have to go over to Garvey."

"Yeah. Shit."

As they walked down Livonia past Betsy Head, D asked for the quick bio on Ice. Since getting out of Rikers two years ago, he had rotated between three residences in Brownsville and East New York. This one housed Shaliya, the mother of two of his five kids. Because of this, Ray Ray figured things would be cool.

Even since D had prevented Ray Ray and two of his buddies from setting fire to a homeless man at the Canal Street subway station, the young man had become a very useful asset to D Security. He wasn't big enough to work the door or do personal security, but Ray Ray knew how to blend in a crowd and let D know when and where trouble might come from. D was proud he'd kept Ray Ray from becoming another African-American statistic, though the kid still knew too many gangstas for his life to be trouble free.

"You don't have to stay," D said as they walked up to the Garvey projects. "Just introduce me to Ice and go."

"And leave you alone? Naw, dog. I don't think that's a good idea."

"Yo!" The voice came from the roof of the nearest Garvey building. It was a youth, maybe seventeen or eighteen, wearing a Yankee cap and a scarlet Cincinnati Reds jacket. "Stay right there." Then he spoke into a cell phone. From the building entrance, two equally young, equally red-garbed youths, came up and, without a word, frisked D and Ray Ray right there on the sidewalk. Ray Ray was going to say something but D shook his head. One of the two, about six feet, rail thin, with yellowed freckled skin, pulled out a Beretta from his waistband and gestured with it for his prisoners to move into the building.

Wordlessly, all four walked past the lobby and up a narrow staircase—the taller Blood in back, the shorter, darker kid, solid as a fullback with big, broad shoulders, leading the way. D's nose filled with familiar scents: rotting food in overflowing garbage bags and fried bananas, piss and pussy, too much perfume and not enough deodorant. For poor folks in cramped living conditions, the smells are always pungent and mixed up like bad gumbo on a Saturday night.

Reaching the roof was a relief for D's nose, though the visual was none too comforting. Three other Bloods, including the kid who'd yelled down—early twenties, cocky, smoking a joint—and a chubby, nondescript man of around thirty who had that flunky vibe. The third man was around fifty. Bald head. Some gray in a beard that was really just a thin line that curled around his cheekbones into a slender mustache. Clearly this was Ice.

He looked at D but spoke to Ray Ray. "This is your man right here?"

"Yeah. This D Hunter."

"So," Ice said, turning to D, "you from 315 Livonia?"

"Yes. Grew up in apartment 6C."

"You know Little Z."

"No. Not personally. But my brother Jah used to speak about him."

"Jah?" Ice surveyed D coolly. "What are the names of your other brothers?"

"Matty and Rashid."

"They both dead, right?"

"Yes. Right on the corner of Livonia and Stone."

"They call it Mother Gaston these days."

"Same damn corner."

Ice took a few steps toward D. "You know, your family's kinda famous around here. At least to people my age. So you made it out. Good for you."

"It's a hell of a way to get a rep."

"True dat. You got the money?"

D reached into his jacket pocket and pulled out a white envelope. He was impressed that neither of the two kids who frisked him had touched the envelope, a sign of discipline in the ranks. Ice gestured to the other older Blood who came over and removed the envelope from D's hand.

"Ray Ray says you can help me."

"Malik Jones. He died in a fire at Rikers about three years ago."

"What about the two kids who stabbed my friend?"

"Can't help you with them. But you ask some of your police friends about Malik Jones."

"What's he got to do with my friend's murder?"

"You gave me some money and I gave you a name. Once you start asking about this man, there'll be no turning back. Right now your friend is dead and you been cut up a couple of times. When you start asking about this man, it'll get more serious for you. But you already know the streets are cold. That's why I gave you this name. I knew Matty and Rashid."

"This Malik Jones has been dead so long."

"True dat. But his life will take you where you wanna go."

Ten minutes later D and Ray Ray were walking toward the Livonia Avenue subway station.

"Ice had mad respect for your family."

"I was a child when they were alive. Don't remember them as well as I'd like." The sirens of an approaching police cruiser silenced them. D turned and watched the car scream down Livonia, under the elevated subway tracks, past the Rockaway station, and down toward the cavernous public housing.

"What next?"

"Ice knows those two kids who stabbed Dwayne. I'm sure of that. But Malik Jones? The name Malik has come up before. Is he just a red herring, a way to guide us away from the two kids? I gotta look this guy up."

"I don't think Ice would have had this meeting if this wasn't real."

"Good point."

"He wanted to check you out. Maybe he'll come back with more."

"Maybe. But don't ask anything else right now. Just lay back. You've already earned your money. I don't want you stabbed up."

"I'm with that."

Ray Ray gave D a hug and then disappeared into Brownsville's darkness.

Standing on the Rockaway platform, D glanced down toward 315 Livonia Avenue. "Malik Jones," he said into his cell.

"Well, now we have a last name," Fly Ty said. "Now it's an actual lead."

After he'd put the cell away and watched the Tilden projects for too long, D turned and walked to the other end of the long platform. Thanks, Brownsville, he thought. Thanks for too damn much.

CHAPTER 16
ROUND THE WAY GIRL

It was a cake gig. All chocolate with vanilla frosting. Every summer Russell Simmons held a soiree at his East Hampton home for his Rush Philanthropic arts foundation called Art for Life. On his large back lawn a huge tent was set up and held dozens of banquet tables, a dais, and a section reserved for a silent auction. You could bid on a night in the studio with a Def Jam artist or ten private yoga sessions at Jivamukti, the popular studio that Russell attended, or an abstract painting by Russell's older brother Danny. All the items reflected the connection between hip hop and the Hamptons that Russell had helped foster in the mid-'90s.

Not surprisingly, the crowd reflected that same cultural merger: chilled-out Hamptons habitues, city folk just in for the weekend, and celebrity drop-in's from fashion, media, and film. The evening had some of the flavor of the event D had worked with Jay-Z months before. But this being the Hamptons and Russell's home, it was considerably more laid back and very low-maintenance for D and his discreetly placed employees. There was the odd paparazzi getting a little too aggressive. Some guy couldn't find his girl and asked D's peeps for help (though D knew she had slipped upstairs with one of Russell's Hollywood pals). Otherwise it was calm and quiet as a country summer night should be.

Aside from keeping the peace even more peaceful, D had another mission this starry July night. He was on the hunt for Amina Warren-

Jones, who ran a Rush Philanthropic Arts–affiliated charity in Newark, a successful catering business in the Oranges, and was one of the most beautiful widows D had ever seen.

If Amina was a candy bar, D thought, she'd be a Hershey's with tasty almond lumps repping her breasts and thighs. She was a lovely chocolate snack of a woman, sort of like Gabrielle Union with the kind of short, wavy hairstyle favored by young Halle Berry. The way she was dressed that day—sundress, dangling earrings, and mules, all in an olive tone—heightened the sensual impact of her brown skin. Amina carried herself with shoulders back and neck straight, as if she was determined to face the world head-on. Long curly lashes framed fierce brown eyes that quickly took your measure and made their judgment. They were smart, intuitive, and pitiless too.

Living with and loving Malik all those years meant she was blissfully unaware of her husband's (mis)deeds, knowing only what she wanted to—either that or Amina was a true blue ride-or-die bitch, a gal with a Beretta in her briefcase and C-4 by the front door. D wanted her to be righteously naïve, but her bearing and those penetrating eyes said the woman knew things. D was kind of afraid to find out what, but knew at some point tonight he'd have to try.

This lovely woman's late husband had been one serious piece of work. Malik Jones, a.k.a. Brother Malik, a.k.a. Jonesy, a.k.a. Marvin Johnson, had had many names and many identities over the past decade plus. He'd been a club promoter, owner/driver for an escort service, manager of singers and MCs, and had a couple of production companies. No felony convictions—just two marijuana possession misdemeanors. The only hint of violence on his rap sheet had proved fatal. He'd been arrested in Manhattan three years earlier when, while traveling with Baby of Cash Money Records, he got into a shouting match with a white businessman and fractured the dude's left cheekbone. It was that fight that led to his incarceration at Rikers, where someone tossed a Molotov cocktail into his cell.

A Google search of images for Malik Jones had found the dead man in the entourages of MCs, as expected, but for a Jersey guy it was a surprise that most were West Coast rappers—Ice Cube, Snoop, Too Short, Dr. Dre, various Dogg Pound members, and several with Suge Knight and Michael Williams, a convicted drug kingpin who'd claimed it was his money that originally founded Death Row Records. Malik had been way deep in the LA rap scene at the height of the West Coast/East Coast wars and seemed squarely on the side of the left coast.

As D ran all this info (much of it gleaned from Fly Ty) through his mind, he found himself hovering around Amina Warren-Jones. She was beautiful and her late husband was, somehow, someway, involved with Dwayne's death. It made for a real intoxicating combo. Still, he shouldn't have been standing so close to the lady as she surveyed a Glen Friedman photo of D.M.C. performing onstage at the Palladium back in the sainted year of our Lord of hip hop, 1985.

Amina suddenly turned and looked D in the eye. "Well," she said.

Caught off guard and feeling completely goofy, D responded, "You're from Jersey, right?"

"That's right. You find that exotic?"

"No. It's not exotic. Not at all."

"That's too bad," she said.

"Really? It's too bad I don't find Jersey exotic? That's crazy."

"It's too bad because it means that after staring at me all night, the best thing you could come up with was, You're from Jersey, right?"

"Whoa. I had more to say than that. Believe me, I did and still do. You just came back with the 'exotic' thing so fast I couldn't get going."

"Well, Mr. Hunter, you need to get started."

"You know my name?"

"Yes, but don't go feeling yourself. I tried to get a friend the contract to do security for this event, but Russell's people had already committed to you. You have a surprisingly good rep for a former doorman."

"Damn. I'm not sure whether to be flattered or insulted. But you knowing that I'm a good dude with a good business can't be a bad thing."

"As you may be aware, I'm here with someone."

"Well, I'm working and probably shouldn't even be speaking to you this way, but—"

"No, you shouldn't be speaking to me this way."

"Okay. But if I hadn't I would have regretted it. And that's a fact."

"You are an earnest type of guy, Mr. Hunter. Some would even say kinda corny."

"Not to my face. Most people would not say that to my face."

"Hmmm. I believe that. And I believe you mean that corny stuff you just said."

"Listen, I'm in security. It's what I do for a living. That means I'm quiet most of the time. I'm not an MC. I'm not slick or any of that fly shit. I do a good job. People respect me. So my question is: are we gonna get together some time?"

"Are you on Facebook?"

"Should I be?"

"If you're a friend of Russell Simmons, you're a friend of mine. I'm in his New Jersey network."

"Will you accept me as a friend?"

Amina smiled sly and amused, and walked away. That hadn't gone as D planned. Not at all. But as soon as he got back to Manhattan, he joined Facebook.

CHAPTER 17
DA ART OF STORYTELLIN' PART 1

D looked down upon Union Square from the second-floor cafeteria of Whole Foods and watched a squad of breakdancers pop, lock, wiggle, spin, and sweat on the long, gray stone steps of the crowded city park. Ever since the World Trade Center attack, when Union Square had become a gathering place for mourners, protesters, and folks desperate for community, D had found himself drawn to this public space, regularly stopping by to observe the chess players, beggars, lovers, haters, capoeira students, painters, jewelry sellers, and gawkers like himself, along with thousands of others who poured out of a subway station that serviced seven lines.

He chewed on curry chicken, brown rice, and cucumber while gazing at a five-man crew, armed with a new version of the old-fashioned ghetto blaster. Though it wasn't a word D used often, the whole thing felt "quaint" to him, like some delicate little vase that had been preserved from antiquity. Maybe up close these were just some funky-smelling young hustlers from the hood (seven brothers and a Puerto Rican gal), but from across a wide avenue and above the park D saw echoes of the city's grimy past.

Even back in the '80s, when Union Square was a haven for junkies and dopemen, breakers armed with cardboard and JVC cassette players had claimed part of the park's real estate. Their painter caps and fat-laced sneakers were as much a part of the city scene as Ed Koch's

"How am I doing?" and once windy, now demolished Shea Stadium.

As he munched on his curry, D watched the young dancers evoke a culture he remembered firsthand. They leaped and twisted their supple, toned bodies, paying homage to a legacy they were claiming and show-casing their athletic prowess. For the tourist, it was legendary New York grit and swagger—which, unknown to them, wasn't nearly as pervasive as back in the day. D mused that to some New Yorkers the past was important only as long as you could charge somebody for a taste of it. If not, just move the fuck on.

Once outside Whole Foods, feet firmly planted on 14th Street, D took in the scene on the ground, watching the vendors crowded along the curb while shoppers brushed by him. He enjoyed all the crazy en-ergy of it, the feeling of being caught in a whirlwind. Then down into the subway station and uptown to a busy day in the enchanted land of new-school hip hop.

D hopped off the N train at clogged Herald Square and walked west past Macy's, Penn Station, and across Eighth Avenue on 34th Street. Despite his large body and black clothes, D got no slack from the women with stuffed plastic shopping bags who bumped and slammed into him as if the security guard was invisible.

So he was quite relieved to arrive at the Hammerstein Ballroom where VH1 was holding its annual Hip Hop Honors broadcast and much of his D Security team was employed for the night. In the lobby D was greeted with hugs and shakes from other beefy men in dark suits, many of whom wore small gold-on-blue D Security lapel buttons, which were awarded to those who'd been down for five years or more.

While D was looking into Dwayne Robinson's death, he had not been neglecting his business. Fear was still paying the bills. In fact, fear was one of the great growth industries of the twenty-first century. The

WTC attack had set the tone for the new millennium, and if you were in any form of the security business, your bills were paid.

At the Hip Hop Honors, the fear was never of the audience, which was made up of recruited kids who stood on the Hammerstein floor and danced and cheered at all the appropriate times. Nor was D worried about the folks sitting in the mezzanine, despite the open bar and tons of record business vets in party mode.

It was the artists themselves who were the biggest source of potential danger. If you were doing security at a hip hop event that brought together MCs from more than one clique, posse, label, hood, city, or region into a single backstage area, your team had to be up on any and all beef, whether announced on AllHipHop.com, proclaimed on a mix tape, or just heard in the VIP section of nightclubs from South Beach to the Meatpacking District.

This year's HHH lineup was rich in possible beef. There were a couple of old-school New York pioneers on the bill, many of whom thought today's upstarts used "Mickey Mouse rhymes" and argued that the young rappers should be "paying a tax to the creators." There were MCs from Atlanta and Miami who gave lip service to "respecting the pioneers," but really didn't give a shit what these graying New Yorkers thought. Luckily, there were no Miami-versus-Atlanta troubles—MCs seemed to move between these two Southern cities with ease.

However, within these two towns there was beef galore. Who was really king of the South? Who was really the boss of MIA? Local beef between artists with national followings could explode into violence if scheduling and security were not well designed. (Trick Daddy was going on early in the evening to keep him away from DJ Khaled and Rick Ross. Though T.I. and Ludacris got along, relations between elements of their entourages were tense.)

These were just a few of the issues D and his team sat discussing at a round table in the basement of the Hammerstein Ballroom. Times of arrival and departure for talent. Where's T.I.'s dressing room? Where's Gucci Mane's dressing room? How do we keep the talent's security guards from eating the crew's meal? The latter sounded like a joke but it was a potentially volatile situation. Teamsters and production staff got agitated when non–crew members, particularly brothers in white T-shirts, filled plates from their dinner-break buffet.

Fisticuffs between teamsters and personal security often jumped off at music video shoots. That could get ugly real quick. So this issue took up a considerable amount of time before the meeting adjourned.

After another quick walk-through, checking out the key entrances and exits for talent on stage right and left, D walked into the high-ceilinged ballroom, gazing up for a minute at the cherubs floating up and then down toward the stage where a rehearsal was in progress. A medley of Atlanta hip hop hits was underway with Asher Roth, a young white MC with a strong college following, negotiating the tricky cadences of Big Boi's rhyme on an Outkast classic. This was dangerous ground for any MC, much less a white kid with only a couple of hits.

The stakes were high for Mr. Roth since this HHH, like every year, the final rehearsal performances were watched by a who's who of MCs coming, going, hanging out, and quietly critiquing their peers. It was D's favorite part of the day, since it was MC on MC, everyone stripped of their pretension and ego. Very communal and also very serious. He'd seen Melle Mel watch LL perform one year and marveled at the two possible rivals giving each other dap. He'd seen Big Daddy Kane perform lazily at a run-through and heard Fab Five Freddy give him a pep talk that may have inspired the most electric performance in the show's history. Today, as Roth walked to the edge of the circular stage, D noticed Bun B, one of the most lyrical Southern rappers, nodding his approval. Roth saw this and they made eye contact, a silent acknowledgment of his skills.

It was a moment that made D remember why he'd once loved hip hop. That exchange wasn't done for a Flip camera or YouTube. It wouldn't be chronicled in the *Source* or blasted across the net via AllHipHop.com. For D it was as genuine as hip hop once was and always should have remained. It made D smile.

His BlackBerry buzzed and he saw a text, a New Jersey number, and his mood grew even lighter. *I'll be there. Can't wait.* It was Amina. She and a girlfriend were coming as his guests and D was giddy. Sure, she was the widow of a mysterious East Coast/West Coast thug who was somehow tied to a close friend's murder.

But damn, she was fine, and they had mad chemistry. D hadn't felt this excited about a woman since his ex Emily some five years ago. If he was really a detective this would be dangerous, but D was just a guy asking questions, a very lonely, curious man. He could make people feel safe. Yet no one held him when he was tired and his tears always dried on their own. His HIV status made relationships complex, but his desire to be loved was so, so elemental.

As the casted audience of good-looking folks filled the orchestra floor and an older group of friends and music biz types sat down in the balcony, D wandered between the television production trucks behind the Hammerstein on 35th Street and the backstage area, listening on his headset to the chatter of production assistants, floor managers, and his security staff. Reports of red-carpet arrivals, delayed town cars, and revised script pages came in nervous waves. The production offices were filling up with marijuana fumes wafting over from a nearby dressing room, which was doing nothing to calm the growing anxiety as the clock moved inexorably toward taping time.

And then D was running toward the stage, excited voices filling his earpiece. "Altercation stage left!" Flo Rida, maker of pop-rap ditties and tall enough to be an NBA point guard, was not happy with DJ Khaled, the de facto king of Miami nightlife, maker of party anthems and close compadre of rap giant (in sales and size) Rick Ross. Along with several associates, the two men were having a heated argument.

During the performance of one of Flo Rida's hits, Khaled, who was DJ/musical director for the medley, had let a recorded voice intone "*Maybach music*" two different times. That "Maybach music" phrase was synonymous with Rick Ross. Flo Rida and his peeps saw this as some kind of dis, while Khaled said it was a simple mistake. Whether intentional or not, D knew that from small disagreements big guns sometimes emerged.

A scrum had formed stage left. There was some scuffling. A few "motherfuckers" had been exchanged. Many hard stares. D arrived. Cooler heads. Calmer words. Beef squashed. A truce for tonight. Back in Miami, who knows? Not D's problem.

The dust-up turned out to be just the prelude to a rocky night at a normally smooth-running show. There was an edge to the evening. Not exactly a mean edge—more like a sense of joyous anxiety, like anything could happen and wouldn't that be fun? Which isn't great for television but is fuel for the fire of a real hip hop show, since it lets the street into the building, connecting the highly professional to the culture's unpolished roots.

Like a boxer, D was on his toes a lot during the taping, bouncing from backstage to the front of the house, admiring how Bow Wow, seemingly too young to understand nostalgia, tapped his childhood for a dynamic version of Kris Kross's "Jump," and being amazed at how enthused a New York crowd could get for Dirty South hits like Juvenile's "Nolia Clap."

D's favorite part of the evening was peeping up into the mezzanine where, looking so sexy she belonged on stage, Amina sat at a front-row table in a low-cut top, gladiator sandals, and brown legs for days. From various angles of the Hammerstein, D gazed over at her, while also clocking her very attractive caramel-colored girlfriend with long braided hair and an older black man, fiftyish, vaguely familiar, who shared the table with them.

Toward the end of the taping, which ultimately looked smoother on the tube than it felt behind the scenes, D moved through the crowd of dancing fans, took a side staircase that carried him past honorees like Luther Campbell, Jermaine Dupri, and the three producers of Atlanta's Dungeon Crew, and then went up to the VIP-laden mezzanine.

People were standing and dancing next to tables (and on a chair or two) as Khaled and Rick Ross, resplendent and ridiculous in a waist-length fur coat, proclaimed "We always win!" from the lip of the Hammerstein stage. Amina, twisting her hips like a snake through sand, waved D over and embraced him warmly.

"I see you're having a good time," he greeted.

"Thanks to you," she said sweetly.

Amina introduced her friend Courteney, who looked even better up close: a light-skinned beauty with her braided hair, very snug blouse, and leather pants over some arresting curves. Courteney shook D's hand and then Amina said, "And you must know this man."

"Amos Pilgrim," D responded. "It's my pleasure."

Pilgrim, a record business legend, one of the heroes of Dwayne Robinson's *The Relentless Beat*, stood next to Courteney, swaying old–black man style, self-conscious about his age but absolutely happy to be there.

Short and dark brown, Amos wore a Rolex with enough diamonds to make Kanye jealous and a well-tailored, casually expensive tan shirt, brown slacks, and leather loafers.

"Hey, my brother," the man said, and took D's right hand into both of his.

"So D," Amina said, "we're going to the Rose Bar for a drink. Please come join us."

"I have some housekeeping to do, but give me an hour and I'll roll by."

She gave D kiss on the cheek. He took in her perfume, hoping some attached to his suit. Except for the Miami performers and their various entourages, most of the acts had already left the building, off to the official after-party and various soirées around town.

As the audience filed out of the building, D and his team locked down the backstage and various dressing rooms, which were scattered in the basement, the eighth floor, and in tour vans parked on 35th Street. Some artists, big dawgz like Timbaland, had never even entered their assigned spaces, rolling in just before taping, lingering a bit backstage, and then SUVing away as soon as their section of the show had taped.

In contrast, many of the less-heralded acts had grabbed water bottles, gobbled down every bag of Doritos, and even swiped a towel or two from the restrooms. For some of the artists on HHH, this was their first national TV appearance and/or first time getting any significant New York City shine, so as far as they were concerned, everything was up for grabs. By the time the team had completed its rounds, D was among the many with a contact high from the variety of herb, chronic, sticky icky (and any other name for marijuana one could employ) that floated through the now empty spaces.

It was more like two hours when D finally arrived at the Rose, a Lexington Avenue hotel bar, which had become an instant Manhattan hot spot when it opened in the early 2000s. The heat on it had cooled, as things do in NYC nightlife, but there were still enough bold-face names in the room to fill half of Page Six. The doorman had once worked for D, so getting in for this black noncelebrity was no hassle.

Though there was no smoking inside, there was a hazy, smoky quality to the room's light. D peered through it, seeing models, Euro-trash, and trustafarians aplenty. Over on one of the Rose Bar's minisofas sat Amos and Courteney, while Amina perched on a stool sipping champagne. Aside from a couple of tall, dark, short-haired models, they were the only black folks in the room. D settled down with them, a bit wary of Amos's reaction since older rich men were never keen on having young, muscular types around when they were getting their cougar on.

But Amos was relaxed and laid back, seriously kicking game to Courteney, who he was impressing with his knowledge of Apple's long-term business plans. Seemed he had a supertight relationship with Steve Jobs and was telling her about their next magical machine. D would have liked to eavesdrop on Amos's info but Amina was picking his brain for gossip.

"And why didn't Janet introduce Jermaine Dupri for his tribute?"

"Hey, I just do security. I'm not privy to every decision."

"Hmmmm, I know you know."

"I really don't. But you're right, that's not info I would volunteer."

"But you'd tell me if you knew, right?"

"Maybe."

"Maybe? Maybe's no way to woo a lady."

"Is that what I'm doing?"

"I thought that was what you were trying to do." They both laughed. "But let me tell you something: I like secrets. You share with me and I share with you."

"Oh," interjected Amos, "what's going on over here."

"My friend D is being a little stingy with the backstage gossip."

"That's the man's job. How can a man do security if he's telling the secrets of the people he's securing. That's not how you keep someone safe."

"Well, you can take his side if you want to, Amos. But one thing I know is that there are no secrets. Not really. Everything done in the dark eventually comes to light."

"Whoa," D said. "That's scary but true."

There was a lull in the conversation, so D jumped in and asked how Amina had met Amos.

"Out in LA, wasn't it?" Amos replied. "You were with Malik."

"Yes, it was some fundraiser out at your place in Malibu." To Courteney she added, "He has an amazing house right on the Pacific. You should see it."

"Perhaps she will," Amos said with a rakish smile.

Amina was clearly in cahoots with Amos. But D's mind wasn't at the Rose Bar; it was on the West Coast. Amina had gone out there with her late husband. She had to have known at least something about his activities. More to ask her about later. Quality time with Ms. Warren-Jones was definitely essential, though he wanted to kiss her more than ask questions. Either way, the ghost of the late Mr. Jones would have to be dealt with.

The ladies needed to head back to Jersey ("Some of us have normal lives," Courteney said more than once, so everyone hopped into Amos's SUV and accompanied the ladies to a Midtown parking lot. While Courteney and Amos had a private car-side conversation, D and Amina spoke a few feet away.

"So I guess my question is, am I gonna see you again?"

"And why wouldn't we see each other?" She was messing with D, batting her eyes and touching his jacket lapel.

"My insecurity, I guess."

"Most men aren't honest enough to admit that."

"Maybe. I don't know about other men, but I was very excited you came."

"Well, I owe you for the tickets. Dinner at my home this weekend?"

That was an easy yes. Hadn't had a home-cooked meal in a long time. They embraced again—this time deeper—and then she signaled over to Courteney, who was still fielding Amos's latest offer. Courteney gave the black millionaire a chaste hug and a peck on the check before the ladies headed back to Jersey.

"How'd you do?" Amos asked after their car had pulled off.

"She invited me over for dinner."

"Nice," he said. "I'm headed down to a spot called Greenhouse on Hudson to meet Andre Harrell and some other people. You wanna roll?"

"Naw. No way. Usually after a show like that I'd be in bed by now."

"I hear that. But I'm gonna stay out. I don't get to New York very often, so I'm gonna run around a bit longer. I've heard lots of good things about you. Feel free to look me up when you next get to LA." Amos handed him a business card with his name and a telephone number embossed on it.

"A card with no e-mail address. That's seriously old school."

"Classic shit remains classic shit."

And then Amos was off to a long night of clubbing, while D walked down Ninth Avenue with the man's card in his breast pocket, Amina's image in his mind's eye, and the lyrics of Southern hip hop songs running through his head.

CHAPTER 18
OTHA FISH

D had never spent much time in Jersey. He'd seen some Nets games back when J Kidd was running the break and he'd bodyguarded a couple of wealthy swells who trekked out to the old Meadowlands Stadium to see U2. Actual time amongst the Garden State's regular folks had been limited to a couple of dinners at Dwayne Robinson's house and a shopping trip to Ikea with his ex Emily.

D had been so worried he'd get lost on the Jersey Turnpike on his way to see Amina Warren-Jones that he was actually a half hour early. He'd driven around a bit, looking at the suburban city in the encroaching darkness, deeming Short Hills not as pretty as Montclair and considerably more livable than rough-and-ready Newark. Looking at some of the black homeowners he spied exiting SUVs and tending to their lawns, D recalled how his mother had dreamed of such a life when they were kids. These days she was living comfortably in Flushing, Queens, with her second husband—but Queens was not as plush as this.

Amina's home was a two-story brick Colonial with a good-sized lawn and a white lawn jockey in front. A late-model BMW sat in the driveway and D parked his rented Lexus behind it. The large man suddenly felt quite nervous, both because he hadn't had a home-cooked meal in years and because instead of this being an interrogation, he was on a date. D's butterflies were so strong he was at risk of mumbling his way through the entire evening. He was about to ring the buzzer when the door opened and Amina, all brown hues and blinding white teeth, looked him up and down.

"Welcome, D."

"Oh, thanks for inviting me." He stood in the doorway and held out two gift-wrapped packages.

"Why thank you. You can come in, you know."

D smiled sheepishly and entered her home, feeling as awkward as a thirteen-year-old on his first date, and also a bit guilty, since this was not, at least for him, a totally social call.

"I brought red wine. I don't actually drink," he said, "but people who do tell me it's a good vintage."

"Okay," she replied, eyeing the large square package under his left arm, "can we share *that*?"

"No," he said with mock seriousness. "This is only for you."

D began unwrapping the brown paper. When he finally pulled out the prize, Amina laughed.

"How'd you get that?"

"I called Rush Arts and found out who'd won the auction. Then I made an offer he couldn't refuse."

"This is amazing." She reached out, kissed D on the cheek, and took possession of the Glen Friedman photo of D.M.C. that they'd both bid on at Russell Simmons's house. Amina held the photo before herself with both hands and then turned and walked into her living room with D on her heels.

The scent of sandalwood incense filled the space, which had a warm beige and bronze color scheme with lots of pillows and a low coffee table by the fireplace. Unlike the tomb D called an apartment, Amina's home felt like a place where you'd chant in Sanskrit and have couscous with lentils for dinner. It had turned out to be an easy place to find and would be a hard place to leave.

Amina had made a vegetarian feast with Indian accents. A huge salad laced with walnuts, raisins, hummus, chickpeas, brown rice, mushrooms, and a thick curry sauce. She'd traveled to an ashram in Goa a couple of times and had picked up a lot of cooking tips when she wasn't chanting or doing backbends.

"Have you ever meditated, D?"

"I guess you could say I do every day. I keep my apartment very dark. Black, really."

"Is that why your wardrobe is so consistent? Coordinating with the wallpaper?"

"Are you making fun of me?"

"No. I always invite undertakers over for dinner. What's the deal with that?"

"Well, it's a story."

"And what else is dinner for?"

So D opened up to her a bit. He hated the instant sympathy the deaths of his three brothers generated in women. It brought out the mother in even the most cynical female and made him, the surviving son, seem a victim, a role he resisted at all costs.

What he rarely told, and wasn't planning to tonight, was that he was HIV-positive. As much he was drawn to Amina, he wasn't going there. Strictly on a need-to-know basis, and despite the obvious chemistry, he didn't think any such revelation was at this point necessary. The tragically true tale of D being the last surviving Hunter son was enough for an introductory meal.

"So that's why the all-black? You are in mourning."

"Yeah."

The story of D, his mother, and brothers made Amina tear up. D didn't cry but made some mighty sad faces. So well before desert they were no longer at the table but hugging each other stretched out before the fireplace.

"I never had any kids," Amina said quietly. "But I did lose my husband. In fact, we weren't married very long before he became more a ghost than a husband."

"Seems like he traveled a lot. Got into a lot of things."

"Yes, Anthony did."

"Anthony? I thought your husband was named Malik."

"Malik Jones. That was his cover name. Anthony Jackson. That's his real name. Actually, Malik was a nickname I gave him. Sometimes he'd get into his black militant moods and I'd call him that."

D's head was swimming now. Malik Jones was Anthony Jackson? His wife had given him the name?

"But your last name is Jones."

"I adopted that to help him out. To keep his cover consistent if someone began checking up on him."

"Cover? You make him sound like some kind of spy."

"I guess he was, in a way."

"Russell told me your husband was kind of a thug."

"And Russell thinks he knows everything. But he doesn't." Amina's tone was more melancholy than angry. "Russell didn't really know him. At the end of the day I didn't know him either." She stood up and offered her hand to D. He rose without a word and let her lead him into the kitchen and through a door that opened to a furnished basement: pool table, leather sofa, video games, and old copies of *Sports Illustrated* and *Forbes* magazine. It was a man's area. There was a light layer of dust, so different than the vibe upstairs.

"This was my husband's space. It's where he could be himself, I guess."

D was looking around when he saw a picture of a man in a uniform. At first glance he thought it might be Anthony Jackson's father or even grandfather. He stepped closer to the photo as Amina smiled.

"That's him when he graduated from the Police Academy."

"Police Academy?"

"First he was a police officer. Then he got recruited by the FBI."

"Wow. That's not what I expected."

"Sometimes the whole thing still surprises me."

"I'm trippin' right now. I really am."

"I debated what I would tell you all day. But it feels right. Especially after what you told me about your family. I guess we're both a little damaged." She came closer to him and wrapped her arms around his waist and placed her head on his wide chest. "Don't hurt me, D, and I won't hurt you."

"I'll do my best."

"You're supposed to say, *I won't hurt you.*"

"I know, but I've seen too much to act like I can control anything, especially the future."

Amina let D go and stared him in the eye. "Okay. I understand that. Would you like some dessert?"

"I'd love it."

As they headed back upstairs, D took a glance back at Jackson/Jones's suburban basement and felt the dead man's ghost glaring at him from the shadows.

Standing in the kitchen as Amina sliced up a vegan sweet potato pie, D said, "Thank you for sharing that."

"You're not the only one who can use Google. I read about you and Dwayne Robinson. I asked Russell about you. After he got over—for about the fourth time—that we weren't gonna sleep together, he said good things about you."

"So Russell Simmons cosigned me?"

"As much as he can for any man closer than he is to getting something he wants."

"Oh. Am I closer?"

"Closer than Russell Simmons doesn't necessarily mean close."

D laughed. "You got jokes."

But he wasn't laughing when she leaned, grabbed him by the head, and kissed him, parting his lips with her tongue and pulling him into her mouth. After a moment, D separated himself and took her by the arms.

"I have to let you know something about me. Something that could change how you feel about me."

"You're HIV-positive, right?"

"Yes."

"I heard some rumors. I asked around. How long?"

"Six years now. I'm not gay. Didn't shoot heroin. Best I can figure, I got it having unsafe sex with a young woman I didn't know. Didn't use a condom. But then it might not have been her. I'm not really sure. Not that it matters at this point. Not at this point."

"You look great."

D explained that he was one of the lucky ones. "Like Magic," he said, "but without the long paper. I was in good shape when I found I had it and I'm in great shape now."

"Yes indeed, you do look good."

Half ignoring Amina's comment, lost in his own confession, D continued: "The 'monster' didn't destroy me. It just made me vulnerable. So every winter I worry about colds. I'm afraid the flu or some allergy will kill me. I'm as strong as a bull, but if I don't take my meds, for whatever reason, I get afraid I'll shrivel up like a raisin."

D was now looking off into the distance, back into the past, to that day at the doctor's office, like it was a scene from *Grey's Anatomy*. When he gazed back at Amina her eyes were swelling, once again heavy with moisture.

"I'm sorry," D said, not knowing what was appropriate. He hadn't told many people. He'd only had one or two girlfriends and a few scattered lovers since he'd been diagnosed six years earlier. His great love, Emily, a mixed-race British party promoter with a taste for Cuban cigars, had taken the revelation well, telling D she had herpes and joking that they made a fine couple of losers. And even when Emily left him for a dreadlocked Jamaican man, D couldn't be mad at her. She'd already been more understanding than he'd ever expected any woman could be.

"You are in such pain, D." Amina reached across the table and held his large hands between her slender fingers. "I bet you don't even understand how guilty you sound."

"Maybe, Amina, but it feels like guilt I deserve. I don't know why."

"Cause your brothers are gone and you're here?"

"Maybe."

"D?"

"Yeah."

"When was the last time you were intimate with someone?"

"With myself. Last night. That's the safest sex I know."

"You wanna come upstairs with me?"

"Would you hold me, Amina? I'd like that."

"I think I can do that," she said.

"I don't want your charity."

"And I don't want yours."

She took him by the hand and led him through the living room and up the staircase to her bedroom, which was as brown and inviting as her living room.

CHAPTER 19
TALKIN' ALL THAT JAZZ

It was three weeks after his dinner with Amina-Warren Jones. Three weeks of pleading Fly Ty to contact the FBI and other feds to squeeze out some intel about undercover operative Anthony Jackson, a.k.a. Malik Jones. Reluctantly, Fly Ty finally agreed to dig deeper into the life and times of this increasingly mysterious man with multiple identities.

Which is why the two men were sitting at a corner table in Balthazar—one of the various Keith McNally–founded bistros that defined high-profile dining in downtown Manhattan—having roasted chicken, oysters, and sundry sides, and sharing a bottle of cognac on D's tab. Fly Ty had demanded a princely meal for all the aggravation that the search for info on Amina's husband entailed. Balthazar had been his choice. Luckily for D, he'd done McNally a service a few years back, so getting a power table wasn't too difficult.

"This was like pulling the layers of skin off an onion," Fly Ty said after a nice rich swallow of Chivas Regal. "People aren't comfortable getting to the core. Besides, it appears only a select group of people knew what Anthony Jackson was into. You ever see *Apocalypse Now*?"

"Yeah. Good movie. Got a little weird at the end."

"As you may remember, at the start of the film a general tells Martin Sheen that Marlon Brando's methods are 'unsound.' That's their bureaucratic way of saying the man was becoming a damn cannibal in

'Nam. Well, according to folks I spoke to, Jackson/Jones's methods were just as unsound."

"*Unsound.* That's some real bureaucratic bullshit. Don't act all cute, Fly Ty. I'm paying, so break it down for me. Who is Anthony Jackson?"

"Well, to start, all that stuff I told you about Malik Jones is both true and totally false. All that stuff I said that Malik Jones did, he did. Now, Anthony Jackson went from beat cop to an NYPD buy-and-bust when Harlem was crack-la-lane. He was decorated for his work and then recruited by the FBI. He started working undercover as a hip hop entrepreneur. Somehow around then he got involved with the Sawyer Group and met your man Dwayne Robinson.

"Because he was so well known in the streets of NYC, Jackson volunteered to work on the West Coast. Then it gets murky. He was assigned to a special unit that interfaced with a number of other units. His smart idea was to pose as a guy from the East Coast who wanted to invest in West Coast rap. In his cover role, Jackson/Jones got involved in record distribution and even got a piece of a record company."

"So he was working for the FBI and clocking dollars on his own."

"Turned out Jackson/Jones was a real good businessman. Along the way he gained the confidence of Freeway Ricky Ross and other figures in the crack trade, helping build cases in conjunction with elements of both LAPD and the Bureau of Alcohol, Tobacco, and Firearms."

"Freeway Rick was all up with the CIA bringing crack into LA, right?"

"I saw that show on BET too," said Fly Ty. "I know as much about that as you do. No one proved a thing. It's just ghetto conjecture."

"Sounds like Malik might have known what was up with that."

"What Malik knew about that or anything else, I have no idea. I do know he helped build a number of cases on the West Coast. Definitely compiled a fat dossier on Death Row. He was so tight with them, he was in the car behind Tupac and Suge that night in Vegas."

"Did he know who did it or speculate on who it was?"

"If he did, it's not in his reports."

"So when did he become 'unsound'?"

"In the year between Tupac's and Biggie's murders, he got in with the rogue cops out in the Rampart Division and stopped turning in regular reports. After Biggie was shot in LA, he went totally underground. No word to his office or his wife."

"Damn, his wife is way too fine to ignore."

"Well, he did for a year. The bureau wanted to bring him in but he refused, and in that year he apparently set up another identity, so he was hard to track. As far as anyone knew he hadn't broken any laws, so they didn't push too hard."

"He could have been dead."

"But he wasn't. At some point he began e-mailing in reports and, despite the bureau's misgivings, the intel was good and played a role in violating a bunch of folks."

"That could have gotten him killed."

Fly Ty took another sip of cognac and nodded at the obvious.

D said, "Sounds to me like he was turning in people who he had his reasons to see incarcerated."

"You're not the only genius out here, D. So the bureau terminated his employment and then mounted a big effort to bring him in. But to their credit, they didn't blow his Malik Jones cover."

"Or kill him."

"Well, they didn't find him. No luck. Radio silence. They put his wife under surveillance. Checked her bank accounts. Nothing. A few years go by. He contacts the bureau. Says he's got info on drug trafficking linked to major hip hop figures in New Orleans, Miami, and Atlanta."

"New Orleans?"

"Yes. Apparently, he'd relocated down South and built a whole new network of music and drug biz contacts. Turns out one of the reasons he'd been so elusive was that he had relationships with local law-enforcement officials in various cities and was slipping them credible info in exchange for money and their silence. And he was obviously spending a lot of time down South."

"They didn't know he was on the run from the FBI?"

"Maybe he was using another identity. It's hard to tell how all that worked. Then Malik Jones gets arrested in New York in a car with some NOLA rappers—loud music and erratic driving on Broadway got them pulled over. They found guns in the car. Malik Jones had an out-standing Cali warrant and gets cuffed. The warrant popped up, but not that the FBI wanted him for questioning. A quirk, I guess. By the time the local bureau found out he was in custody, someone lit his ass on fire."

"So it was a hit on him?"

"He shared a cell with a Blood member named Anfernee Brown, a vicious street thug who'd been charged with all manner of mayhem. A lot of people didn't like Anfernee. It's possible Malik was in the wrong bed at the wrong time. The other possibility is one of the old school–loving heads at Rikers hated crunk and mistook Malik for one of those country rappers."

"You sayin' he got killed for crunk?"

"Some of those guys been in the system so long they think KRS-One is still hot . . . You know, when they finally buried him it was with a closed casket."

"Fly Ty, this is the second time you've told me this man's life story, and it's hard to believe either version."

"Yeah, together or separate, they are quite a tale. But I don't think they bring you any closer to finding who killed your friend."

"You know what's missing? His posse. There's no way he did all this stuff in the street, both as a hustler and a cop, without someone helping him."

Fly Ty asked, "What about the wife?"

"She didn't have to tell me her husband was an undercover cop."

"So that means she's clean? Maybe it just means she wants to confess. Maybe she really likes you. And wouldn't that be sad?"

"Women still like me," D smiled. "And I've had *the conversation* with her."

"Okay. You both got your cards on the table. Good for you both. You may get a girlfriend out of this but I'm not so sure it'll get you a murderer."

That night D had another dream.

He was looking out of the front window of a 3 train as it rose from a tunnel into sunlight. D was both the little boy that he'd once been and the man he was now, each standing next to each other like a father and son, as the subway car rolled into and out of the Rutland Road station. It moved with great speed around the bend through Saratoga and Rockaway avenues.

Between Rockaway and Junius Street, the train stopped suddenly across from the Samuel J. Tilden projects. From a side window the two D Hunters could see apartment 6C, where his mother, all dressed in black, peered out of her bedroom window down at the street.

At the corner of Mother Gaston and Livonia, under the elevated tracks, train wheels shrieked and engines grinded, and older and younger D, dressed in vanilla suits perfect for Puff's white party, stood before three wreathes, a dozen candles, hand-written condolence cards, a dirty Adidas shell toe, a pair of Clarks Wallabees, black Tims, a deflated basketball, an unopened golden Trojan package, a Black Panther comic book, and a stack of twelve-inch singles with the Stop the Violence Movement's "Self-Destruction" on top. Old D reached down and handed "Self-Destruction" to young D, who snapped it like a potato chip in his small hands and laughed.

CHAPTER 20
THINGS DONE CHANGED

Ever since D was a boy in the hood, he'd possessed a sixth sense about being watched with bad intentions, and he'd learned to trust it the hard way. When he was ten, two teenagers yoked him from behind in a smelly project staircase and bloodied him pretty good. D knew he'd felt something coming down those stairs but had been so fixated on getting to a Mister Softee truck, he'd ignored the feeling of being clocked through a cracked staircase door. Not paying proper attention had cost him his ice-cream money, a bloody bottom lip, and a bruised collarbone. He never ignored that vibe again.

So, as soon as he exited the subway at Broadway and Lafayette, D knew eyes were on him. Between the legion of shoppers ogling the bare-chested male models in front of the Hollister store, the vendors hawking caps, ice cream, and bracelets, and the wave of shoppers rolling down toward Soho, this intersection was as crowded as any in the city. D's ghetto Spidey sense was tingling and he looked left and right, mostly seeing scores of females with shopping bags. Then someone bumped into him from behind. He turned and spied two young black men with flat-fronted baseball caps, diamonds in their ears, skinny jeans, and multicolored kicks. Immediately D recognized they were students at the high school for gay teens up on Astor Place. One said, "Excuse me," politely, while the other said something flirtatious.

Deciding there was no point lingering, D continued down Broadway toward his office at 580. In the elevator he was joined by three female yogis headed up to Virayoga, located on the floor below his office. Sussanah, a comely little brunette instructor, dressed in orange-and-green flowing yoga gear, flip-flops, and a charming smile, chatted him up.

"It's time you came downstairs and took a class. It'll be great for your stress." She squeezed his arm. "Obviously you lift weights, but your energy always seems a bit blocked to me."

"It has been hectic lately."

"I heard about what happened."

"Yeah. It was bad."

"All the more reason to come to a class," she said with practiced calm. "It'll help you connect to your breath, and that's something you can draw on any time."

"I hear you," D replied, thinking that watching Sussanah twist up her prêt little body while they both sweated would probably keep him tense. She gave him a class schedule before exiting and he watched her tight yoga booty as the door closed. He laughed as he thought of himself stretched out on a rubber matt with Sussanah guiding his body into pretzel-like shapes.

His smile faded as the door opened onto the site of Dwayne Robinson's death. It became an outright scowl when he saw the building's super and two white men in suits standing at D Security's door.

"William, what's going on here?"

All three men turned as D approached. The older of the two white men, maybe forty-five, already gray on top with a matching silver mustache and a Long Island accent, reached into his pocket and pulled out a badge.

"Agent Robert Van Winkle, FBI."

Van Winkle sat on the other side of D's desk, while Aubrey Graham, thirtyish and silent, sat off to the side, taking notes and occasionally nodding. "So," Van Winkle began, "we know you've been trying to find your friend's murderers. I personally respect your efforts. That's what I'd do if I thought NYPD wasn't really following through. Now, I take it you feel this Sawyer memorandum is some kind of key to the attack on him."

"Before we go any further, can I know why Dwayne Robinson's death interests the FBI?"

"Aubrey," Van Winkle said, "step outside for a minute, could you?"

The younger agent nodded and left the room wordlessly. D thought it was a nice bit of theater, creating a false intimacy between D and the remaining agent. Alone with D, the man pulled out his BlackBerry, scrolled through it, and then handed it across the desk. On the screen was a photo taken in winter of Dwayne Robinson in an overcoat and wool cap, talking animatedly with a tall white man wearing shades, a Russian fur hat, and an oversized parka.

"Scroll across."

D did as he was instructed and saw that in the following five pictures the conversation became more animated, and by the last one the man had pushed Dwayne to the ground.

"Who's the white dude?"

"He's not familiar to you?"

"No. Who is he?"

Ignoring D's question Van Winkle said, "You were the last person to see Dwayne Robinson alive. I read the police report but wanted to meet you myself."

"To see if I knew this guy."

"But you don't?"

"I'd sure like to."

Van Winkle stared at D, sizing him up. "Mr. Robinson's murder is unfortunate, but it's not the reason I'm here today. Mr. Robinson had some dealings with the man in these pictures. His name is Eric Mayer."

"I know that name," D replied. "He used to promote parties around New York. A lot of stuff in the Hamptons. He never hired me to do any of his events so I don't know him personally. Maybe we met in passing."

"As far as you know, Mr. Robinson and Mr. Mayer had no business dealings?"

"I mean, I never heard Dwayne mention him. Dwayne was more a historian than in the mix these days. So hanging at hot parties in the Hamptons wouldn't have interested him. I have no idea why they'd be in contact."

"Okay, Mr. Hunter."

"Is that it?"

"Unless you know more about Mr. Robinson and Mr. Mayer's relationship."

"What did this man do that would interest the FBI?"

"Violations of numerous statutes involving interstate commerce."

"Smuggling."

"Yes."

"Of what?"

"Thank you for your time, Mr. Hunter."

"Do you know anything about an ex-agent named Anthony Jackson—sometimes known as Malik Jones?"

"No."

"You know who I'm talking about?"

"No. Does this Jackson have something to do with Mr. Robinson's death?"

"Somehow, though he's been dead three years or so."

Van Winkle lifted his BlackBerry off D's desk and typed on the keyboard. "I'll make a note of his name." There was a pause. D expected him to get up, but the agent lingered. "You know people in this hip hop world. People who'd trust you more than an FBI agent. Some tip about Mr. Mayer might come your way. If it does, let me know." Van Winkle handed his business card to D and stood up.

"You haven't given me much information to go on."

"Sounds to me like you already have a lot on your plate," Van Winkle replied, ending the discussion.

And then he was gone, leaving D to wonder what the conversation meant. Seemed like the FBI agent didn't know about Jackson/Jones. Could Van Winkle really know less than Fly Ty? Still, he definitely wanted D to go after Eric Mayer. No question about that. Those photos fired him up just as Van Winkle knew they would. Interstate commerce? What was that a euphemism for? If it was drugs, he would have said so. Guns? Cigarettes?

D Googled Eric Mayer and was surprised to find that the man's hip hop career was pretty deep. He'd actually been involved with several labels, including Profile (home of Run-D.M.C.), and managed a few acts too, before getting brands like Xbox and Sony Playstation to house hip hop–themed gigs for rich white rap aficionados. He had even partnered with Diddy and Jessica Rosenblum on parties in the Hamptons, Manhattan, Vegas, and Miami. There were photos online of Mayer tossing back champagne with Penny Marshall, Paris Hilton, Adrien Brody, and other hip hop Hamptons habitues during the '90s and early '00s.

There wasn't much online about Eric Mayer after 2005, though there was a 2007 item in Page Six about a charity he started to bring technology to inner-city youth. What made D's eyes widen was the charity's name: the Sawyer Foundation. According to a short profile in *Hamptons* magazine, Mayer was a big fan of Mark Twain's *The Adventures of Tom Sawyer*; he explained how the book had a natural connection to today's youth: *"The style of Twain's writing is colloquial and raw, like that of a great MC."*

D hadn't read *Tom Sawyer* since fourth grade and wasn't gonna start now. He skimmed the summary on Wikipedia and didn't really see anything too interesting about it. Then he noticed the name Huck Finn in the text and remembered that there had been some racial issues with the book, that some black parents had wanted it banned from school back in the day. He looked up the summary of *The Adventures of Huckleberry Finn* and the name Nigger Jim jumped off the page. Jim was a big, raw, ignorant brother who shared a raft on the Mississippi River with a little white boy who helped him survive. It was a leap to see Mayer as a modern-day Huck Finn, but this weird throwback reference to Sawyer made D uneasy.

CHAPTER 21
AS THE RHYME GOES ON

D was in a meeting with a representative from Sprite and a commercial production company when his BlackBerry buzzed in his pocket. He was gonna ignore it but the meeting was winding down and he felt certain that his company would be providing security at the shoot in Los Angeles in the next few weeks. So he took a peek.

The text was from Danielle Robinson: *Good news. I found part of Dwayne's book. Please come see me.*

After wrapping up the meeting as quickly as he could without seeming rude, D had a brief talk with Danielle and ordered a town car. Ninety minutes later he sat on the Robinsons' living room sofa looking down on four composition books stacked on an end table. Good old black-and-white books with lined pages that generations of American children had utilized for readin', writin', and 'rifmatic. On the cover of each, Dwayne Robinson had written his name, a year, and a month. Paperclips bound sections of the composition books together.

"He wrote everything in these kind of notebooks," Danielle said. "Often he'd rip out pages he'd written on, type them into his computer, then tear them up and toss them out. Usually the only things left in them were his diary entries." She paused. D said nothing, figuring this was her first time expressing any of this out loud. "He would stack them up in a box in the bottom of our bedroom closet. I guess that's why that thief didn't find them. They go back years—some to when he was in college. I've been reading them lately." Another pause. "There are a lot of lovely things in his diaries about you."

"Me?"

"Yes. He loved talking to you. Said you kept him in the mix."

"He was such a cool guy. Always teaching, you know?"

"When I was reading through the notes, I found some pages that I think are from *The Plot Against Hip Hop*. Sometimes you can't make out what he's written—it looked like chicken scratch when he really got going. But maybe you can get a sense of the book from them. Maybe there's some kind of clue."

"You think so?"

"I do, but I'm not a hip hop fan like you and Dwayne. What I can see is that he really did believe there was a conspiracy to try and manipulate hip hop culture. He describes some pretty terrible things. How he knew them and what he could prove, I don't know. I supported his writing but didn't pry. Maybe I should have."

"C'mon, Danielle."

"No. I'm all right. You read these books." She stood up. "Let me know what you think. Just go to where the paperclips are and you'll see the *Plot* sections."

As soon as Danielle left, D grabbed the book dated *September 2009* :

Is there any question hip hop is dead when the hottest young rap star is from Canada and the dude has a bum knee? What's that got to do with trading verses, break beats, and ciphers? That's right. Zero. On the strength. Word. There's no shooting the gift anymore. No one's going for mine trooper. I don't think anyone's kept it real since maybe 1997.

Nas was right (as he often is) and hip hop is as dead as Cow-

boy, T.R.O.Y., Eazy-E, Biggie, and Pac. But I'm afraid it's too late to revive the body. Gone like eight tracks, hi-top fades, and Sugarhill records. And I've found the perpetrators. What follows is the record of my investigations, which constitutes a secret history of hip hop.

A few pages later there was another fragment from what sounded like the introduction:

The thing about conspiracies that people don't understand is that they never run as planned, that even when the goal is achieved there are usually a raft of unintended consequences—and that the wider the conspiracy, the more likely it wasn't a real conspiracy but a single well-planned event followed by a series of fortunate accidents.

So to destroy or change something is not to make it disappear or obliterate it completely. The idea is to alter its DNA so that a person, institution, or movement evolves in ways that benefit the manipulator and, fundamentally, undermine the original principals. So a well-designed conspiracy is one that takes the long view and identifies forces that can be manipulated without having to formally engage them in one's enterprise.

This was it for that particular notebook. The next one was dated November 2009. It felt like it was the end of a chapter.

Their network of operatives was wide and easy to manipulate. In the world of hip hop, which was just a microcosm of black America, people were anxious to get paid, needy for fellowship, and extremely jealous of those more successful than themselves. These character traits, all connected to a stunning sense of insecurity, made the plotter's job very easy.

Within every organization in hip hop, from Def Jam to Death Row, from Bad Boy to Cash Money, there were folks who thought they were smarter or more hood than whomever they worked for. Even before the phrases "hater" and "hateration" (the latter courtesy of Mary J. Blige) became ghetto staples, this tendency amongst black folks to envy those more successful made manipulation of people and events quite easy.

The conspiracy never demanded that nonprofessionals do bad things. Anything serious that had to be carried out (murder, assault) was never ordered by the conspiracy. Wasn't necessary. Now, that's not to say that sometimes people in this world didn't get overzealous when given certain information. You give hungry, ill-educated people a thought, a suggestion that someone who's more successful than them looked down on them or joked about them or even complained about their attitude, well, that often results in bad decisions. I guarantee you that some of hip hop's greatest MCs and businesspeople who could have snookered P. Diddy are in jail for overreacting to a bit of news they should have shrugged off.

Truth be told, for every street thug who became a manager capable of working with Williams Morris and CAA, for every gangbanger who Microsoft would be comfortable making a deal with, there were five hundred brothers and sisters who were emotionally and psychologically incapable of stepping out of the hood. So it didn't take much skullduggery to control hip hop. It was just a matter of helping the most volatile people in on the game rise to positions of prominence. Eventually they'd sabotage themselves and, in so doing, bring down scores of others. Insecurity leads to incompetence leads to negligence leads to obsolescence.

In *December 2009* D found a few pages he assumed were from some-where in the middle of the manuscript. The heading on the top of the page was *(S)ucker*.

The lady's name was C. Delores Tucker, and she was somebody's idea of a force to push back against the wave of hip hop washing over the nation. She was the kind of fallen civil rights–era hero the black community was full of in the '80s. Years after the movement's peak they'd fanned out into corporate America and political positions, in-creasingly isolated from the people they'd worked to serve and quietly prosperous in a comfortably middle-American way. They still liked to march—police shootings and candlelight vigils were their special-ties. The civil rights generation, however, didn't know jack about economic empowerment other than government programs, while the hip hop generation, for better and worse, was consumed with stack-ing chips. This led to a profound disconnect between them.

As the hip hop generation's power grew and disrespectful record-ings became popular, some factions within the conspiracy thought a full frontal assault would cool its ascendance. So, according to multiple sources, a Los Angeles–based businessman with ties to the conspiracy identified C. Delores Tucker as a perfect tool for an operation to impact the distribution of hip hop music. The former Pennsylvania attorney general was recruited to be a spokesperson for antirap views, while several other women from the black music business were employed as well.

She was seen as a much more viable voice than Bob Dole or Tipper Gore, Al's old lady, who had jump-started the labeling of recorded music with the creation of the PMRC (Parents Music Re-

source Center). Tipper had initially organized the group after being outraged by Prince's "Darling Nikki" and some heavy metal records. But a whisper or two in her ear and the delivery of lyric sheets of Ice-T to her Georgetown residence, and gangsta rap became public enemy number one.

An angry old black grandmother was the perfect mouthpiece.

And that was that. Whatever else the writer thought about Tucker and her highly publicized campaign, including congressional hearings that Dwayne Robinson himself had testified at, was missing.

The final composition book was dated *January 2010*. It was the longest section and the most chilling.

The agents behind this conspiracy weren't heartless, totally immoral men. There's evidence to suggest that, if properly motivated, they could have done something close to the right thing. One of the many hip hop moguls of the '90s was getting desperate. His empire was crumbling. Hitmaking producers were jumping ship. Attorneys were trying to weasel artists out of their contracts. So he called a label-wide meeting, demanding that everyone under contract and their representatives show up.

At this meeting Malik Jones was present. He was acting as manager/advisor to one of the acts. The label boss sat at the head of the conference room table, gloating Godfather-like, before announcing that anyone who wanted to leave the label was welcome to their release. "If you don't feel loyal to me or this family, that's your choice."

Now, the artists on this label, a hardened group of gang-affiliated MCs, knew a setup when they heard one and sat mute or murmured insincere words of support. A young vocalist, however, barely legal and very full of himself, spoke up. The kid had sung the hook on a couple of hits, had been waiting since junior high for his shot at a solo album. He announced that he wanted his freedom.

The mogul smiled, agreeing to release this fool from his obligation. Then he nodded to two of his "staff members"—big-bodied boys with bad breath and worse intentions—who came from out of a corner and snatched the singer up like a rag doll. "You can leave—no problem—but you must pay the tax." One of the staffers unzipped his pants as the other pinned the singer to the conference table. The unzipped man pulled out his dick and yanked down the young man's pants and, with a frightening glee, butt-fucked him right in front of everyone. Jones did nothing. He was as surprised at anyone at this brutality. He didn't want to blow his cover, but as he watched it, Jones knew he was now complicit in something horrible.

The staff member, finally satisfied, pulled out as the young singer's tears filled the conference room table. Some of the women in room cried and most of the men sat back, embarrassed for the singer, though at least one attorney found it funny.

The room emptied quickly. The mogul had made his point. Jones left with the others, mute as a mummy but knowing this event was the crossing of some line. He knew that no matter what he was ordered to do or what made strategic sense, this mogul had to go down.

D closed the book and slumped back against the sofa. This was seriously dark stuff. Definitely the kind of info that got journalists threatened and maybe killed. Malik Jones, it appeared, was likely a partial source. This last excerpt suggested that Malik had perhaps, to some degree, cooperated with Dwayne. Maybe that tape was an earlier conversation? Maybe Malik was murdered at Rikers because of this operation? Or, D thought, am I just like Dwayne, or even Truegod: finding a few threads and knitting a blanket.

He peered back down at the composition books and realized they were adding one more layer of frustration to his life. The writing was both precise and vague. Dwayne obviously knew a lot of things and had talked to a lot of people, but aside from Malik Jones and C. Delores Tucker, there were no names mentioned. Who was the LA businessman? Who was that rap mogul? There were so many things suggested, yet so much missing. It made the whole reading experience feel very hollow.

These were early drafts, tiny pieces of a larger whole that was as lost as a 747 in the Bermuda Triangle. Between the Sawyer memorandum, the cassette tape of Dwayne and Malik, and these manuscript slices, D felt like he was in some Spielberg movie—*D Hunter and the Search for the Hip Hop Documents*. Yet D had no whip and there was no swashbuckling going on. Just an accumulation of things that one day, one way, could *maybe* add up to something useful.

D had hung out on several lazy Sundays in this living room, watching sports and talking hip hop and life, which made reading his friend's work even more poignant. He was tempted to peek into the non-*Plot* sections of the composition books, to hear Dwayne's voice toss off sociological observations like some folks breathe. Dwayne and Danielle had never had any kids, so in that space they'd developed myriad friendships with young people they cared about—nieces and nephews, students and mentees. Dwayne had even joked once that he ran his very own Motown-style artist-development program, where the goal wasn't to turn out a Diana Ross or a Marvin Gaye, but sharp, observant, analytical young people. Dwayne had been taught to *think* (writing being a pure projection of the mind) by great editors and he sought to share that passion.

D wished that he was smarter, that he had the skills to pull all the pieces together in his mind, the way Dwayne did in all his books. Instead, he was just a big man who was employed because *tall, dark, and scary* had currency in the culture. He wasn't the brute that some saw when they glanced his way, but their view of his body and face paid the bills. It didn't matter what he was—only what they saw.

The first tear fell down on the cover of the *January 2010* composition book. It was big and fat, and splashed when it landed. D searched around for a napkin and ended up using a blank sheet of paper from one of the books to blot his eyes and wipe his tear off the book's cover.

There was a bathroom on the first floor by the kitchen. He headed there quickly, not wanting the widow to see him bawling. Once safely inside, D sat on the fluffy commode top and cried more silent tears, as much for himself as for Dwayne.

CHAPTER 22
CAN'T TRUSS IT

D was packing for California when Pete Nash called with good news. "We know the guy who killed Dwayne Robinson."

"Oh shit," D said, "when did this happen?"

"I've been tracking the case since we talked a couple of months back. Been asking around. It all came together in the last week."

"You said 'the guy'? Thought it was two guys who attacked Dwayne."

"Well, it seems like one kid did all the heavy lifting and the other was more there to help corner your friend."

"You have this guy in custody? I'd love to talk with him."

"Unfortunately he's dead."

"What the fuck?"

"Yeah, pisses me off too. Tracy Morrow was shot out on Pennsylvania Avenue in East New York the other night as he tried to steal a bike from Percy Miller, a ten-year-old kid. Turned out Percy Senior, an off-duty housing cop, came out of their home just as Morrow wrestled the bike from his son. Morrow pulled a knife, and in defense of his son's life, Senior fired his revolver once, fatally wounding the assailant. Subsequent DNA test found traces of Dwayne Robinson's blood on the knife."

"Excuse me for saying this, but he could have bought or stolen that knife."

"Of course, D. But when the detectives from that precinct began talking with Tracy Morrow's associates, one of them, a juvenile named Kenny Parker of the nearby Pink Houses, made an offer: he said if his brother Chris Parker, who was in Greenhaven on a B&E rap, was given early parole, he could connect Morrow to a murder. He claimed to be an eyewitness to a stabbing in lower Manhattan. He knew enough detail to convince a couple of DAs that he was talking about the Robinson murder. It came together pretty quickly."

"Where is this kid now?"

"Somewhere with his family."

"Can I talk to him?"

"Neither of us can. He's underage. But the case has been closed and everyone is happy."

"I really need to speak to that kid."

"D, we have the murder weapon, DNA, and a credible eyewitness. That's as good as it gets for a murder case in this city."

"And what about a motive?"

"This isn't rocket science, or the Illuminati for that matter. It was supposed to be some kid's gang initiation, but he froze up once they cornered Robinson and I guess Morrow wanted to show him how it's done."

"I dunno."

"Listen. You've been thinking a lot about your friend's death. What did his last words mean? What about his mysterious unfinished book? Sometimes a thing is just what it looks like. Hey, you should be happy."

"I guess."

"You know from watching cable that if a case isn't closed in forty-eight hours or so, then most times we never find the murderer. The fact that the killer still had the same knife on him and then got his cap pulled like that is a fucking miracle. At least his wife will have some closure."

"Has someone called her yet?"

"Earlier today someone from the Manhattan DA's office did. D, I gotta go. Big show at the Garden tonight. Jay-Z and a bunch of guest MCs. Okay, D?"

"Yeah."

It didn't feel right to D. Was it all over? One phone call and it's a wrap? Maybe it was two cases: Dwayne's murder and the suppression of his books. Maybe the book stuff only started after his death with the robbery at his widow's house. He wanted to call Fly Ty but the man was on vacation in Jamaica and, with the case officially closed, what was he gonna do from MoBay anyway?

In D's dream that night, he was in the front row of a classroom. A teacher was writing on a blackboard with his back to D. There were no other students—just row upon row of empty chairs stretching to infinity. The teacher, a tall black man in a tweed jacket with leather patches at the elbows, wrote in a very precise script, each letter linked with a chain of curlicued elegance.

Cash rules everything around me. Hard times are sweeping just like the flu. Broken glass everywhere. If it ain't ruff, it ain't right. Jesus walks. Let's define the word called dope. Too cold, too cold. Are you the journal or the journalist? I told you I'd be true. You can't fade me. All I need is one mike.

The teacher filled one blackboard panel and moved over to the next.

The overweight lover. The GZA. Hova. Uncle L. Louie Vuitton

Don. The nigger you love to hate. The Ruler's back. Esco. Weezy. Jeezy. Puffy. Puff. Puff Daddy. Diddy. Rev. Run. Cowboy, T-Roy, Jam Master. Eazy. Pac. Me.

The teacher faced D now and it was Dwayne Robinson. He smiled, cockeyed and corny. Behind his nerdy black-rimmed glasses, his eyes shined red as candy apples. D attempted to question him but no words escaped his lips. Dwayne returned to the blackboard and wrote in a hand perfect for greeting cards.

It was the joint until it was fresh and was stooped fresh, then stooped, then it cold got dumb, unless it was cold chillin' in a hot spot with Big Willie's so supa fly they used beepers to order their sky pagers and mobile phones, which they kept next to their BlackBerry when they weren't shootin' the gift with their Saturday night specials, Desert Eagles, and Mossberg twelve-shot guns at sucka MC bitin' their stylee, while they hated on new swing and busted caps to the north, the south, the east, and the west.

Dwayne faced D again, his smile as radiant as a child. To his left was LL Cool J, bare-chested, seventeen, dukey gold rope and red Kangol garbed, and to his right Notorious B.I.G., massive in a multicolored Coogi sweater and black cap, diamond pendant around his neck. Both LL and Biggie moved their lips very slowly, as if D was an idiot, and said in tandem, "I'm going back to Cali."

Then Dwayne's head fell off and bounced with one big hop into D's lap.

CHAPTER 23
CRANK THAT

D couldn't tell if he was old or just had good taste in hip hop. As he stood watching two Memphis born-and-bred rappers ("rappers" because D couldn't bring himself to think of them as MCs) rhyme about Sprite, the black-clad bodyguard decided it was both. KAG (a.k.a. Kountry Azz Gangzterz) were good dudes. They donned diamond-studded medallions, exposed underwear, the tat "sleeves," but the members of KAG were both publicly married, claimed all their kids were from their spouses, and were planning on buying their mothers matching homes in the Tennessee countryside.

Still, D couldn't overcome his prejudice. Despite the duo having sold millions of ringtones, listening to them made him yearn for real MC skillz. At his most generous, D gave them credit for making infectious dance records with sung/harmonized/rhymed hooks. But the verses were as empty of wit and art as any back-in-the-day disco record. In D's humble opinion, the era of Tupac and Biggie had given way to lesser sing-song rap, just as great '70s funk (Earth, Wind & Fire, the Ohio Players, Kool and the Gang) had yielded to dreck like the Salsoul Orchestra and Cerrone. D figured no one he said this to would get the references, but in his heart he knew the comparison was on point. Not that life would reward him for being a smart-ass. After all, old-school purist or not, on this day he was their employee.

"Hey, bruth," Sneezy, one of KAG's two members, said between takes. "Walk my seed over to the restroom for me, okay?"

D nodded. Sprite was paying him a ton to stand on a soundstage in Los Angeles, so why not? Normally, he would have said it wasn't his job and advised one of KAG's "roadies" to come out of the trailer, put down the blunt, and escort the "seed" to pee. But D felt sorry for Tobe (pronounced too-bee), a roly-poly seven-year-old who'd been stationed by the craft services table all day stuffing himself with enough sugar to fill a wedding cake. So he took the child, who had a head shaped like a football, by the hand and guided him to the restrooms at the far end of the soundstage. D worried that Tobe, who in keeping with family tradition had a huge diamond-studded necklace weighing down his head, would tip over onto his face if not steadied properly. There was no doubt in D's mind that without his guidance those diamonds would swing into the urinal and pull Tobe with them, leading maybe just to embarrassment, but quite possibly a drowning.

So to preserve the boy's dignity and maybe his life, D walked Tobe away from the buzz of the set, past the wardrobe trailer and various pieces of metal equipment. The men's room had an aroma of light mildew and bleach, an unpleasant mix that was nonetheless superior to that of so many public toilets.

"It stinks," Tobe observed.

"Don't breathe then," D said. "Now, you know what to do, right?

Tobe nodded, then walked up to the urinal and unzipped his Rocawear jeans. The kid was just tall enough that he could piss over the lip of the urinal. He was also just awkward enough to almost hit the back side of the medallion around his neck. D walked over to pull the medallion around to Tobe's back when the bathroom door opened.

"You do it all, huh, D Hunter?" The voice was dry, amused, sarcastic, and decidedly white.

D turned to see a thick-necked, square-jawed man with the bleached-white spiky blond hair of a surfer and the Oakley shades of a jock. He had a strong athletic body squeezed into a fairly expensive dark-blue business suit.

"Excuse me," D said as he moved between Tobe and the imposing, self-satisfied man in the doorway.

"I just meant it was cool to see someone dedicated to all aspects of his job. You don't see that much these days. It's a new century, yet professional standards are slipping all over the place. No wonder the Chinese are gonna kick our ass."

"You finished, Tobe?"

"Yeah, I'm good," the boy replied.

"Okay. Wash your hands."

As Tobe walked to the sinks, D shifted over with him, never turning his back toward the stranger. He reached down and scooped Tobe up with his left arm so the boy could get soap and turn on the faucet, while still leaving his right hand free.

"Got your hands full, don't you, D?"

"Do I know you?"

"No. I know *you*." The stranger didn't move, just stood there a step inside the doorway. His hands were folded at his waist in front of him. D decided the man had a military background. Marine. Navy Seal. Something that made him confident and strategic. He moved in to talk only when Tobe was splitting D's concentration. He'd probably been watching D for a while and picked his moment wisely.

D set Tobe back on his two feet and gave him some paper towels to wipe his little hands.

"So," D asked, "are you gonna move out of the way?"

The stranger ignored the question. "It's good, you keeping that little ghetto boy clean."

Tobe piped up and said, "I ain't no little ghetto boy! I'm a balla."

The stranger continued without acknowledging the kid: "Wouldn't want him to catch a deadly virus or any kind of disease. Bet his father and all your other very enlightened clients wouldn't feel safe having an HIV carrier watching their backs."

"HIV?" It was Tobe. "You talking about 'the package'?"

"Yeah, ghetto boy," the stranger continued, "the package. D, you gonna tell him it means you shouldn't have unprotected sex with widows?"

It wasn't what he said, but the tone of his voice that shook Tobe. His petulance faded. Something was wrong. The little boy could feel that D was shook. "I wanna go see my daddy," he said.

D didn't say a thing. He needed to get his bearings. Finally he spoke: "Okay. You tell me who killed Dwayne Robinson and I'll go away."

The stranger grinned. He held up his wrist and looked at his watch. "You better call your office, D. Bad things happen to a man who doesn't mind his business."

Tobe headed toward the door, toward the stranger. D grabbed him by his narrow shoulders.

"You better make that call," the stranger said, then turned and walked away.

D placed Tobe behind him and walked to the door, looking both ways before exiting back out onto the soundstage. And then his phone rang. Fly Ty's voice flowed into his ear.

"D? Brother, you got robbed. Both your office and your house. Both tore up and cleaned out. You need to come back to New York and let us know what was taken."

"I'll be there tomorrow. I'll take the red-eye."

D saw the stranger about to head out the door of the soundstage into the LA sunshine. He could run and try to grab him. But he still had Tobe next to him and maybe there were other folks around with bad intentions. Get the boy to the KAG posse. Then sort out his life.

D took Tobe's little left hand and led him back toward the lights, camera, and action. With his other hand he speed dialed Amina on his BlackBerry.

"Hey, D," she said, "so good to hear from you. You coming home soon?"

"I'll take a red-eye tonight."

"So when will you come back over to Jersey? We miss you over here."

"I have some weird news."

"What's wrong?"

"I think your home is bugged. Maybe even a camera."

"Why would anyone do a thing like that?"

"I think you probably know."

"I'll see you tomorrow then," she said, and hung up.

Back at the set, all was right with the world. Rappers rapped for their pay. Beermakers hawked their brew. Directors went over storyboards and met with advertising agency reps. Everyone got paid. D took it all in, his body back on the job and his troubled spirit far away.

D returned to the Standard on Sunset about one a.m., after dropping the KAG crew off at the W in Hollywood and handing them over to a local man, who'd accompany them on a club crawl into the netherworld of after-hours joints and Hollywood Hills parties. D didn't realize that anything was wrong in his room until he'd shed his clothes, taken a shower, and was brushing his teeth.

Usually the Standard's cleaning staff placed his pill bottles right next to his deodorant and aftershave. Not tonight. A hasty inspection of his bags and pockets revealed his HIV medications were not in his room. Not good, but hardly fatal. They could have easily mixed some poison in with his meds and deaded him. This seemed like just another warning. He could go a day without his meds. They had to have known that.

D laid back on the long bed, looked up at the ceiling, and fell asleep, but only after jamming a chair under the doorknob.

CHAPTER 24
WHAT YOU KNOW

Jersey was beginning to appeal to D. Between his trips to Dwayne's house and out here to Amina's, the Garden State was growing on him. He'd been in his Manhattan cave for so many years that he'd forgotten (actually never known) how it felt to experience a life not dominated by noise, hustle, and concrete. He was even falling in love with Newark Airport, which felt more user friendly than JFK. He had to admit that driving, something he'd only done sparingly in his life, was okay (though he was sure he didn't have the patience to regularly survive rush hour).

Now, as he drove his rental Lexus close to Amina's house, he contemplated buying a car. D was surprised that even after that threat in Los Angeles, he felt so positive. Amina made all the bad stuff out West seem like background noise. It was his mother's words, often spoken and seldom paid attention to, that came to him: "There's nothing better for a silly man than to have a good woman to come home to."

The only dark cloud in his sunny thoughts was that Amina hadn't answered her phone since he landed. It was 8:42 a.m., so she should have been up already and anxious to see him too.

As soon as he turned onto Amina's block, he saw the ambulance and police car in front of her house. The ambulance had run over a few of her flowers. Instead of rushing into the house, D sat behind the wheel, somehow already knowing he was too late. An officer came out, walked over, and asked his name. It didn't go well after that.

Fly Ty didn't know anyone in that neck of the Jersey woods, so D had to sit alone through the long hours of questioning and the looks and the dark sense of guilt and dread that filled his mind. This was so much bigger than hip hop.

"So," said one of the detectives, "that's what you believe?"

"You asked me what I thought," D said emphatically.

The detective, white, thirties, sandy-haired, and portly, looked over his shoulder at his older partner, short, black, forties, who leaned against the wall before turning back toward D. "You have AIDS for seven years. You know unprotected sex would put her at risk. You don't tell her you're positive. She gets infected. She gets depressed. She kills herself."

"Well," D replied, glancing back forth between the two men, "that didn't happen. I didn't infect her. I didn't lie to her. I would never do that. Plus, I don't believe that's why she killed herself—*if* she killed herself."

"So someone else, not you, gave her the virus?"

"That's all I can imagine."

"Homicide by AIDS is not unheard of, and you can be charged for it."

"I would never do a thing to hurt her. Have you checked her body for it yet?"

"We will," the older black cop said, "but this whole conspiracy-against-hip-hop thing doesn't help your credibility."

"It's the only thing that makes sense to me. I know it sounds crazy. But while I've been investigating my friend's murder, people have been dying around me."

"All right," the older detective replied, "okay."

D wasn't sure what that meant. *Okay, I believe you. Okay, I believe you believe that crap. Okay, I'm hungry and it's time for dinner.* Whatever the black detective thought, he tapped the white one on the shoulder and they left the room. About two hours later they released D into a bright Jersey afternoon and to his thoughts.

There was an empty bottle of sleeping pills and a scrawled note by the bed when the Jamaican cleaning woman found the body. Was Eric Mayer behind this? He'd gotten that warning in LA, but why Amina? They'd had great sex but he never penetrated her. He'd been more like a very muscular lesbian lover. Maybe Mayer was an insane man on a rampage, but it felt like there was another player in this game. And if so, Amina's death was it for him. He was through with it. He just wanted to get back to his dungeon.

CHAPTER 25
SOUL SURVIVOR

There was a damn conspiracy. They took it from us, kid. It used to be about skillz. A nigga like me on the mike droppin' knowledge and shit. Now they got these mush-mouthed bamas all over the videos saying nursery rhymes. If I did 'Humpty Dumpty' over a beat I'd be displaying more lyrical content than these country motherfuckas! Sheet!"

D was in the wings at the BET Awards taping at Shrine Auditorium, standing in front of an old-school icon from the Boogie Down as he yelled at Ludacris on stage. What had set this brother off was Luda at the center of a tribute to old-school hip hop, intoning Kurtis Blow's classic "The Breaks" before an adoring crowd of black celebs.

The man wasn't just ranting because of the diamond-studded MC's presence (though he was definitely offended by the Southern MC performing an old-school rap). The other half was that D was unsympathetic and was threatening to have him thrown out of the building.

"Brother, if you do not shut up and leave this area I will have you removed," D told him.

The old-school MC continued on, undeterred. Despite the gray in his locks, the bags under his eyes, and the paunch that was his belly, the man still had some fire left. "How you gonna talk that way to me! How you gonna talk that way to me! I was there before this shit even had a name. But can I get on stage? These motherfuckers wouldn't know real hip hop if it hit them in the mouth!"

And then, of course, he took a swing at D, which the security guard deftly avoided before grabbing the MC and wrapping him in a bear hug, as other members of his team rushed over.

"You all right, D?"

"I'm good. I'm good. Just make sure you don't hurt him."

"Fuck you, D! Fuck you!" the MC screamed as he was led away.

D watched this ugly scene with his hands at his sides. He could smell the bad cologne and the sweat of his attacker on his clothes. Years ago, when D had been a bouncer and the MC was a legend in New York, they'd see each other all the time. Back then the MC had a hi-top fade, dukey gold, and always a fly girl or two by his side. Now he was an angry, not-quite-middle-aged man who'd somehow found himself backstage at an event he probably should have been honored at (at least he thought so).

D felt his pain, but there was nothing he could do. BET was paying him to keep the peace and that's what he was gonna do, as sad as it made him.

On stage, Wale and Kid Kudi had joined Luda in performing a series of old-school hits in a bout of hip hop nostalgia. Nicki Minaj was in the wings, a few feet from D, getting ready to perform Roxanne Shanté's "Roxanne's Revenge."

It was a month after Amina's death. D hadn't been indicted. The death had been deemed a suicide. He hadn't been invited to the funeral, though. It had all been a disaster. A woman he cared about was gone and no one out in Jersey gave a damn about his theories other than to eye him suspiciously and tell him to stay the hell out of their town.

Now he was back in Cali, working at the BET Awards, getting a nice check, and trying to figure out what to do with his life. The old-school MC's rant brought back a lot bad feelings about all he'd heard and learned and what little he could prove. He'd been in Los Angeles for several weeks. Part of it was getting away from New York and thoughts of Amina. Part of it was heading back to the place where he might be able to provoke whoever came to the set of the KAG video shoot, stole his meds, and somehow drove Amina to kill herself.

But nothing had happened. Not a weird look or an off-color remark or anyone trying to intimidate him via words or deeds. Except for the angry MC, the evening had been uneventful. He was just a hired gun at the BET Awards and not a supervisor, so once the last award had been given out and the last limousine had pulled away, D was out the door.

The awards taping ended at five p.m. and D skipped the official after-party and ended up in the Hollywood Hills, at a sexy purple-themed house, for Prince Rogers Nelson's semiannual post–awards show house party. By getting there early, D avoided the cars stacked up on the soon-to-be-impassable canyon roads and got a leg up on the glittering, gifted, gassed-up gaggle of black star power who would be arriving after their courtesy appearances at the BET soiree. Even better, D was not working. He was just another guest.

So he sat cross-legged on the floor as Mavis Staples sang "I'll Take You There" with Prince on bass, D'Angelo on keyboards, and some talented kid on guitar who D didn't recognize but greatly enjoyed. It was the most fun he'd had in a very long time. Just good music played by exquisite musicians for fun (and reputation) at a impressive place full of famous people, none of whom D was obligated to give a damn about.

Then his BlackBerry buzzed in his jacket pocket. It was a text from an unexpected source: *Come to my house 4 a special after party. Amos.* This was followed by a Malibu address. He hadn't seen Amos Pilgrim since that night with Amina so many months ago. It seemed like a cool thing to do.

CHAPTER 26
ALL OF THE LIGHTS

Amos Pilgrim's house was on the beach out in Malibu, a few doors down from David Geffen's and a stone's throw from producer Brian Grazer's. From the Pacific Coast Highway, the house was obscured by a nondescript long, tall, white fence, as anonymous as beachfront property can be. Seven security cameras discreetly lined the wall with only two covering the entrance. Other than that, you'd never suspect that a sprawling three-story Colonial house sat behind the wall, a bit of sturdy New England construction bordering the Pacific.

Inside, Amos's walls were decorated with an impressive collection of African art, along with the odd African-influenced Picasso or other unusual painting hung in between. There were no gold or platinum records or framed posters or anything to suggest that Amos Pilgrim's career stretched back to the age of soul or that he'd advised most of black entertainment's power brokers on career moves and tax shelters. After the celebrity muscle of Prince's house party, this event was more low-key, but hummed with the subtext that this was an event for movers and shakers. Amos was deep in conversation with some older white dude who had something to do with cell phone contracts in Asia, so D wandered over to a window and stood there, transfixed, watching the Pacific lap up against the California shore.

As Marvin Gaye's *Here, My Dear* album played quietly in the background, D smiled to himself and sipped mint tea. It had always tripped him out to be near the Pacific Ocean. He'd often gone to Coney Island as a kid and now, somehow, he'd made it from one end of America to the other, a journey very few of the people he grew up with would ever make. Hell, D thought, some of the folks I grew up with never left Brownsville, much less made it out of Brooklyn.

Yet there he was, sipping on some high-quality herbal tea with Marvin Gaye crooning in the expensively decorated home of a legendary black man. This had to be someone else's life.

"You a tea drinker, huh, D?"

There was Amos Pilgrim, standing arm-in-arm with a gorgeous Asian girl in an aqua slip dress with matching heels and dangling gold earrings. D didn't want to be disrespectful, so he did his best to look at Amos, though the contrast between him and the young lady made it extremely difficult. Since D had last seen Amos, he had put on some weight. He had a scruffy white beard and a patch of bald skin on top of his head surrounded by a crown of graying hair. His eyes were sleepy, his lips red and thick, and his clothes expensive but seemed a sloppy fit. If this wasn't his house and this fine-ass girl wasn't on his arm, you'd think Amos was, perhaps, a well-paid gardener. Compared to their meeting at Hip Hop Honors, he looked unhealthy.

"I don't drink much alcohol, sir."

"So I hear. Well, welcome to my home anyway," he said. Then he followed D's gaze and chuckled. "This is Vanessa. She's what I like to call a black-a-pina."

"Stop that, Amos," she scolded him gently, then explained that her mother was Filipina and her father was black. "Amos came up with that name. I don't like it too much but Amos thinks he can categorize everything and everyone."

"Maybe I can't," Amos replied, "but I do like to try."

"I hear you," D said back, more because he wasn't sure what to say next than because he understood what Amos and Vanessa were getting at.

Amos chuckled and said, "You know, we should talk."

"Any time you'd like."

"Fine. Let's sit down right now. Vanessa, make sure these people are okay while I go have a chat with D. You good with that?"

"Only if you two come back." She kissed Amos on his bald spot, smiled at D, and moved away.

Amos took him by the arm and guided him out of the room. D felt the eyes of many at the party on them, probably wondering why Amos was being so chummy with a bodyguard when there were so many more important people anxious for quality time with their host. D was wondering the same thing.

They turned into a long hallway of polished wood and paintings. "You know who Romare Bearden is?"

"I've heard of him. This is his work?"

"His *Migration* series." There were about ten paintings on each side of the hallway. Inky black figures against verdant green backgrounds. "Bearden wanted to capture the journey of our people from the South to the North. We went from a rural people to an industrialized race. Northern factories needed unskilled labor and they recruited us, D. It changed us too. Never been the same since. Never will be the same again."

"My parents came from Virginia and took the Greyhound bus to New York."

"Mine went from Mississippi to Chicago. But I became myself out here in Hollywood, D. Made a pretty good life for myself in this place."

"No doubt."

"And all I've ever wanted to do was to make sure as many of us as possible could follow my example."

"That's what everybody says, man. They say you give back."

"That's good to hear. What else have you got in this world, really, but your reputation?"

They came to a large metallic door and Amos entered a security code into a wall panel. There was a clicking sound and Amos pushed the door open to a room that looked like a funky bar from the era of platform shoes. In contrast to the more refined ambiance of the rest of the house, this den was all red and black, like the label on the Johnnie Walker bottles set up behind the red leather–trimmed bar on one side of the room. On the other side was a wall of framed photos, large and small, of Amos with Curtis Mayfield, Muhammad Ali, young Jesse "I Am Somebody" Jackson, Don Cornelius, a slender, very sexy Chaka Khan, and a bunch of other bushy-haired, bell-bottomed folks D didn't recognize.

"This is who you really are, isn't it?" he asked in a tone that suggested he'd been let in on a secret.

"Guess you could say that, though the rest of the house is me too. They just reflect different parts of me. Have a seat."

Amos sat behind a battered old dark wood desk and D took a seat across from him in a lumpy black leather chair, which felt like an artifact from the no-money-down furniture stores in every ghetto he'd ever seen. The contrast between the elegant and the tacky in Amos's home was so stark that D wondered for a moment if the old man was schizophrenic.

"I knew Dwayne Robinson," Amos said, which immediately brought D back to the here and now. "He was a nice guy and a damn good writer. His was a loss that affects everyone who loves black music."

"Yeah," D agreed and nodded, though suddenly he felt very cold. He could feel that Amos was gonna tell him something about Dwayne's death, something only a person with his wealth and contacts could know. The idea scared D.

"You probably didn't know that Dwayne did some work for me."

D said he didn't.

"Yeah. First it was a bio or two for some acts I was involved with. He even wrote a speech for a black congressman I was supporting. But the main thing he did for me was this."

Amos reached into a drawer, pulled out a pile of papers, and tossed them on the desk. D picked them up, looked at the cover sheet, and then put them down, as if they were cursed, which, in a profound way, they were. It was a clean, freshly printed version of the Sawyer memorandum.

"I commissioned it and had Dwayne come on board to help shape it. Think I paid him the most money he'd ever made at that point. More than he got for writing *The Relentless Beat*, for sure."

"Why is he dead?" D stood up, his voice and body language menacing, all his reverence for the man evaporated in that instant. D wanted to ask, *Why did you have him killed?* but that might be premature or, hopefully, wrong. Yet he damn well knew Amos had the answer to *Why?*

"Figured you'd want to get right down to it," Amos said, seemingly not at all stressed by the other man's anger.

D figured there were probably eight cameras on him and two retired Mossad operatives ready to come down from the ceiling. So he just stood there waiting for more, steeling himself for the worst.

"To a degree, you could say Dwayne got himself killed, but I'm not gonna blame him for having a conscience. He just made a couple of dangerous people uncomfortable. Just like you have."

"If you brought me into your fucking museum to threaten me, fuck you. I don't scare easy." Now D didn't care about the cameras or the security team on their way to snatch him up. He'd kill the fat old bastard if he had to.

Amos stood up with his palms outstretched in a calming gesture. "I know how fearless you are, D. That's why you're here. I know you're gonna face this head-on. That's what you've been trying to do, but you didn't know enough to do it right. If you died of that virus you got, that would be one thing, right? But if you died over something you didn't totally understand, well, what the fuck would that be? A waste, right? I don't want you to waste another moment of your life."

D knew this was prime-quality bullshit. No wonder this fat little black man had so much juice. He could really run his red lips. "All right," D nearly shouted. "You commissioned the memorandum. You hired Dwayne. You obviously knew Malik and he worked for you too. So why does a twenty-year-old pile of paper get people killed?"

The portly businessman sat back down behind his desk and gestured with his hands for D to do likewise. Slowly D backed down, but tried not to plop into the seat. He wanted to ease in slowly, with control. Instead, he almost tripped moving backward into the leather chair.

Amos didn't laugh (though it did seem to amuse him) cause he had a long story to share. "What I'm about to tell you," he began, "will change everything you think about hip hop and, maybe, your life."

D sighed and slumped deeper into the worn leather chair.

CHAPTER 27

THE SCENARIO

Right after Run-D.M.C.'s hit with 'Walk This Way,' I commissioned the Sawyer Group to create a detailed report on the nature, marketability, and long-term potential of hip hop culture. It took them eight months, but soon as that document came across my desk, I read it cover to cover. Your man Robinson had a nice, very direct prose style.

"At the time I was in a unique position in the industry. I'd carved out a place as the black person white boys at the record labels looked to for recommendations on new executive talent and for who producers/songwriters should make label deals with. If a black attorney or young junior exec at the black music department was ready to take a leap, or if an up-and-coming producer was thirsty for his own distributed label, they came to me and I made sure someone at Sony, RCA, Warner Bros., or PolyGram was aware. If there was a deal to be made, I'd put it in motion. Sometimes I negotiated the whole thing; sometimes I just took a piece and played the background."

"You were what, the black godfather of R&B?"

"Call it what you will. But I had a lot of influence and I used it wisely."

"How'd you get to be that man?"

"Money. I was a generous contributor to both Democrats and Republicans in Cali and around the country. I gave to Jesse in '84 and '88, and I gave to Ronnie in '84 and to Bush I in '88. All the labels' corporate parents were in bed with politicians for their other businesses. I had the ability to speak to both sides. My rep for having influence trickled down to every level of the record game."

"But you didn't believe in anything, did you?"

"No, young man, I believed in *everything*. I was for civil rights and for free-flowing capitalism too. I could feel both affirmative action and supply-side economics. I wasn't ashamed to call Orrin Hatch or Teddy Kennedy my friend. I saw the flow of history and was pragmatic in floating down that river."

"And hip hop scared you, didn't it?"

"The rough part of being in LA is that sometimes you can't see past the 5 highway. It didn't scare me, but it did surprise me. And all the other corporate gate keepers out here too. But I was determined to catch up. The fact that it had an explicit, and implicit, political edge, that it had produced Chuck D and KRS-One, and was engaged with the Nation of Islam and the antiapartheid movement, made my antenna stand up. It was connecting the dots in a way that R&B hadn't since the '70s."

"And that worried you?"

"It worried all of us."

"Us?"

"All the black folks who mattered. All the black folks who'd given our sweat and, in some cases, lives to open the few doors that were already open. This wasn't gonna be the Panthers again—smart young brothers with some good ideas who lost themselves in macho shit. This time we were gonna give them direction."

"What do you mean?"

"Well, through my contacts in the GOP I got wind of the fact that one of the researchers of the Sawyer memorandum, a Malik Jones, was actually an undercover FBI agent working the angle that hip hop was a convenient cover for arms transportation, drug smuggling, and other illegal forms of interstate commerce. So I got in touch with Malik, who by then was living in Ladera Heights, and made him an offer."

"Be your eyes and ears."

"Yes."

"He'd feed you info and you'd use your contacts to help him seem more credible in the industry. It doesn't sound so bad on the surface. But obviously it got out of hand."

"Yes." A long pause. "Two things happened. The first was that Malik began to like playing gangsta more than playing record mogul. Right alongside his pals in the Rampart Division, he began to be seduced, just like everyone, I guess, by the fucking splendor of gangsterdom. Suge Knight had been my bodyguard at one point. I hooked Malik up with Suge during the time that, at my suggestion, we began moving Dr. Dre over to Interscope."

"Cause you were down with the Interscope crew."

"Just doing business. You see, I'd been a part owner of Macola Records, who distributed almost all the West Coast rap in that early period. That guy who owned Ruthless began acting like he was actually running things. Tried to renege on a deal we had for ownership of Ruthless and a bigger piece of the NWA pie. So I had Malik and Suge pull NWA away from Ruthless. Everyone thinks it was about Suge and Eazy. It was really about a business deal gone bad.

"Anyway, I became a silent partner in Priority, who signed Cube once he left NWA. My main goal was to control, one way or another, Ruthless' assets, which was basically Dre and Cube."

"But putting Malik with Suge and the whole West Coast gangsta rap scene eventually bit you in the ass."

"I got the marks here on my right butt cheek."

"Okay. What was this other element you mentioned?"

"I had my hooks into the emerging West Coast scene when that was about to blow. But you can't really claim hip hop—at least you couldn't at that time—without a New York presence. It was still the core of the culture—it was still where hit acts were being created. Malik, though he was from Jersey, was now too West Coast–identified to work as a source/agent back east. On his recommendation we approached Eric Mayer, a very able, street-smart guy from Englewood who was a Jersey state policeman at the time. He'd been something of a wigger before the term even existed. And he was Jewish."

"How did that help?"

"The New York record business, from the corporate offices on Sixth Avenue to the indie labels downtown, was either owned or corun by young Jewish guys. Shit, Russell Simmons didn't have a bar mitzvah but most folks who knew him back then swore he wore a yarmulke under his fishing cap. All his partners were young Jewish guys. So I needed someone who could roll with them, get their confidence, and learn their secrets and vulnerabilities. Eric was perfect. He really was the suburban kid seduced by the culture. By his first summer on the job Malik was reporting to me that Eric was in the mix, he was playing basketball in the Hamptons with Russell. So now I had well-connected operatives on both coasts. But where Malik became too gangsta, Eric went native too. He saw East Coast hip hop as his true calling. Though it was in some weird neocon-meets–old school way I still don't understand. And over time he started his own marketing company, started throwing his own events . . ."

"And you lost control."

"I wish it was that simple. For six years or so, I had both Malik and Eric listening to me, feeding me info while I helped them make strategic moves. We guided Death Row to Interscope. We helped Russ and Lyor move Def Jam to PolyGram after the Sony deal went sour. You wanna know why Suge never went after Russell like he did Puff? Cause between Malik and Eric, I made sure that didn't happen. I was making so much dough off both, I didn't need the grief. We even gave seed money to that Gibbs in New York who sets up MCs with brands. We were the silent hand of capitalism behind hip hop's growth in the '90s."

"What happened to the politics?"

"You tell me. The political acts started making bad records. Simple as that."

"Simple as that, huh? So did you have anything to do with crack coming into the hood? I mean, that's what really changed everything—the culture and the music."

"I had nothing to do with that. Not personally."

"But you were involved with the government. With the FBI and, maybe, the CIA. C'mon. You gonna come clean or not?"

"In the early '80s, a few entrepreneurs in Texas identified building and maintaining prisons as a great business for a spread-out state with lots of small towns. Construction jobs. Food and laundry supplies. Uniforms. The prisoners can work for third world wages. Motels for visitors. Car rentals. The economic benefits went on and on."

"But they needed a way to fill these new prisons up."

"Right. Freebasing was popular out here and in a few other parts of the country for a while."

"Richard Pryor."

"Yeah. Coke was expensive, so you needed money if you were just gonna sit there and cook it all day. But when the crack thing started to happen, you had the perfect storm—an addictive, crime-inducing product, a demand for more prisons, and, along with that, mandatory sentencing for possession of small amounts of crack rock. So it wasn't some simple CIA plot. It was a group of like-minded individuals in Texas, California, and Colombia who came together and connected these dots."

"And you were one of these individuals."

"No. I would never have helped these people do what they did. I knew about them but, honestly, they were too powerful, too connected. God will punish them for this, just like He will for what happened to Tupac and Biggie."

"Go on."

"Eventually Malik and Eric became competitive. Very competitive. One was on the West Coast but had his secret life—"

"And wife."

"Yeah. Well, they both wanted a piece of Tupac. He was connected to both coasts. He had political ties to old-school nationalists and gangsta ties to all the color-coded fools out here. For me, Tupac could have been the political leader hip hop seemed destined to produce. If he'd made it to thirty-five he'd have been a movie star. If he'd made it to forty-five he'd have been the leader of his own international diaspora political movement. One Saturday afternoon he sat right where you're sitting and told me his dreams. I was gonna make it happen for him. I was gonna raise the money, make the connects, and over time set up his future. He was gonna be my legacy. I knew in my soul that Tupac was why hip hop was invented. To nurture that young man and make him the leader that would bring it all together."

"Sounds like a beautiful plan."

"Malik didn't like it. He was jealous of me anointing Tupac. He acted like a child. Maybe he'd become too close to the business and had internalized contempt for artists. I don't know. He feared Tupac, and I believe Malik definitely contemplated having Tupac killed. Now Eric, who'd become this East Coast loyalist, came to hate Pac after he began attacking Diddy, Biggie, and all these folks he loved."

"Seems a stupid reason to have someone killed."

"For some white boy who really wanted to prove something to himself, it somehow made perfect sense. By '95 Malik and Eric were so deep into their own individual journeys, either could have had it done."

"Not together?"

"I don't think so. Possible, I guess, but I don't think so."

"And Biggie?"

"That was definitely arranged by Malik and his Rampart scumbags. Eric had been friends with Diddy since the Jodeci era and this was Malik's way to send a giant fuck-you his way."

"This is crazy shit."

"People always look for complex motives in conspiracies. All it really takes to change history is a few individuals with enough money to buy obedience, enough insight to identify weakness, and the will to do terrible things. Malik is dead but Eric is very alive. That bastard is part of my legacy too."

"So it was Eric who had Dwayne killed?"

"Yes. That I'm sure of. He thought Malik had cooperated with your friend's book and was afraid of being exposed. No doubt about that. I'll tell you something else."

"What now?"

"All those East Coast Bloods you've been getting the last few years? Well, Eric's been selling them guns. It's his way of still having some influence on the street. Gun dealing is how he's kept his hand in, even after New York hip hop became kinda irrelevant."

"Why? He must have made a ton of money."

"Having power and influence is a bigger drug than coke or pussy. Believe me, I know. Listen—if you ever find the two kids who stabbed your friends, I bet they'll be in possession of some shiny new guns."

"Like Berettas?"

"Like Berettas. Desert Eagles. Whatever niggas can kill other niggas with."

"Is that it? Is that everything?"

"Hell no. There's a lot more. We could talk about Nas versus Jay-Z. Cash Money. Why is 50 Cent's entire career predicated on dissin' other MCs? Who placed the gun in Lil Wayne's car that got him a bid at Rikers, and who benefitted from his absence from the marketplace? The waves of shit we set in motion are still rippling."

"All started with one silly report my friend wrote for a couple thousand dollars."

"Yes. That did it. I had the money. I had the contacts and a vision for black people. I'd seen white men shape history and I wanted to do that as well. But niggas are a hard bunch to control. So when I realized I couldn't control them, I tried to guide them. When I couldn't do that, I decided to just take what I could get."

"How can I believe a word of this?"

"Don't be stupid, D. You think white men are the only ones who can play chess?"

"You told me all this cause one day I'd come after you for Dwayne's murder."

"Nigga, please," Amos said with a bitter laugh. "You giving yourself a little too much credit. If I hadn't told you all this, you'd still be looking around Brownsville for two kids with box cutters."

"Okay, motherfucker: why?"

"Cause . . ." Amos paused and suddenly looked sad. "Cause, just like you, I'm dying a little every day. I have inoperable colon cancer—just like every other black man who ate too much pork and smoked too many Kools. Got a year. Maybe eighteen months. Your HIV ass will probably still be here when I'm gone—but only if you're real smart."

"It's that white guy, right? The one I met at the commercial shoot. Looked real military. He's the FBI guy."

"No. He was probably just a guy paid to fuck with you. All I know is that Eric's made a lot of money and done a whole lot of dirt. Motherfucker's resourceful when it suits him. He's got the same quality Phil Jackson has—he knows how to get talented black people to do his bidding, even if it's sticking a knife in someone's neck."

"All this shit you've told me, I don't know what to believe."

"It's your choice. Everybody can't process the truth when they hear it."

"I should kill you. How about that? For Dwayne, for Amina, and the people I don't know who are dead because you wanted to turn a dime into a dollar."

"Maybe you should. Would save me some time. But you won't. Besides, that wouldn't stop Eric. It would just make him happy. One less thing to worry about."

D stood up, leaned across Amos's desk, and snatched the older man up like a sack of dirty laundry. He stared into the man's frightened eyes a moment and then reared back and drove his right fist into the center of Amos's face, sending him backward with a broken nose. He landed hard on the ground and his head snapped back against a chair.

D looked down at the moaning, crumpled body of Amos Pilgrim and seriously contemplated finishing the job. He breathed heavy and heard his heartbeat. It wouldn't take much. D's fist was sore and flecked with blood.

The murderous impulse passed. His breathing slowed. Amos said something but D had heard enough and was out the door and back in the living room before he realized how much trouble he'd be in if Pilgrim pressed charges.

Once back on the Pacific Coast Highway, D made a strategic decision. He MapQuested LAX and looked at his watch. Only nine-thirty. By ten-thirty he was sitting in a business class seat on a red-eye back to New York.

CHAPTER 28
IT'S LIKE THAT

The plane was sitting on the tarmac at JFK and anxious New Yorkers awaited the beep that signaled the race to open the overhead baggage compartments. D flicked on his BlackBerry, not sure what message would be awaiting him about his roughing up of Amos Pilgrim.

Nothing from the left coast, but many a missive from his man Ray Ray. *Ice needs to see you. Get at me.* There were four of them. *12:40 a.m., 1:15 a.m., 3:02 a.m., 4 a.m.* D called from the plane but got Ray Ray's voicemail. While in baggage claim the return call came through, Ray Ray's tired voice was as sad as a tear.

The taxi driver didn't want a shorty, especially to where D had to go, but once inside the vehicle there was no removing his sleepy, irritated, angry self. The destination was not Manhattan, but an uninspiring patch of Brooklyn bordering Jamaica Bay known as Canarsie. Named after Indians, the remote area in southern Brooklyn had been home base to nearly every ethnic group to pass through the city except Native Americans—Jews, Italians, Southern blacks, Jamaicans, Trinidadians, Russians, and more. Tightly packed homes with street-level garages and narrow backyards dominated the area, and it was in front of just such a nondescript house that D emerged from the taxi and, bags in hand, walked up a stone staircase.

The buzzer said *S. Compare*, but the sleepy-eyed teenager who peered at D through the glass looked more Latino than Creole. He opened the door without a word and D entered. The place looked like it had once housed a nice working-class family—a plastic-covered sofa, framed family pictures on the walls and end tables. But fast food wrappers, discarded cigarettes, and the stench of men who rarely showered suggested its current life was a flophouse.

"I gotta frisk you," the teen said, the first words he'd uttered. D put down his travel bag and suitcase and submitted to a very rudimentary search. Down a staircase into a carless garage, D followed the youth, knowing whatever was down there wouldn't pretty.

"What up?" Ice said. D stopped at the bottom of the steps. "Hope you had a nice flight."

Strapped up with belts and rope in a makeshift electric chair was a bloody, tattered, hollow-faced, and defeated Eric Mayer. Wires were clipped to his right and left wrists, his bare feet, and somewhere between his legs that D decided not to look at too closely. They were all hooked up to an electric contraption with bad intentions.

"You know this man?"

"Eric Mayer," D said, not moving any closer.

"Not Rico Drayton or Andre Young?" Ice pulled a wallet out of his back pocket and leafed through credit cards and various fake documents. "This white man has a lot of black-sounding names."

D finally walked over to Mayer, studying him the way scientists do a frog they plan to dissect.

"How'd you find him?"

"I didn't. Fool was looking for *me*."

Ice stepped to Mayer with an open palm and slapped him into semiconsciousness. Mayer groaned and a bubble of blood popped out of his split lips.

"Motherfucker was going around the Ville acting like he was welfare and he had benefits or something for me. One of my kids had bought guns off him awhile back. Sometimes he'd work out of a place on Atlantic." Ice produced a big Jamaican spliff. "You want some?"

"Not before breakfast."

Ice fired up the joint and inhaled deeply before speaking again. "After I snatched him, I took a picture of him and sent it around to a few niggas. It came back that he was the fool who hired those kids to wet up your friend. Two thousand—a G apiece. But they say *he* really killed the man." Ice reached behind his back and pulled a revolver out of the waistband of his quite visible Fruit of the Looms. "You wanna handle this?"

D pulled out his wallet and offered Ice $900 in cash. Ice held out the gun as he took another puff. Spliff still between his lips, he took the money.

"I'll have Ray Ray deliver the rest."

"No rush," Ice said. "I know you're good for it."

"You sure this man is the killer and not the two kids?"

Ice shrugged. "This is as close to justice as I can offer. And definitely all you can afford."

D walked over so close to Mayer he could smell the funk of the beaten man's loose bowels. "Why did you kill Amina Jones?" Mayer's eyes were red—at least what D could make out through the puffy, bruised eyelids. The question seemed to actually amuse Mayer.

"Well, well, well." That was all the beaten man said.

D didn't like Mayer's flippancy and punched him dead in the mouth, loosening several front teeth and sending the chair he was tied to down to the garage floor. He stood over Mayer and peered at his bloody knuckles.

"Don't you worry about anything else." Ice stood next to him and patted his shoulder reassuringly, a gesture that made D feel complicit in a way that disgusted him. "Jamaica Bay is a few blocks away."

D nodded and headed back upstairs.

Canarsie was the last stop on the L train, a subway line associated in the twenty-first century with hipsters who got off in Williamsburg and Bushwick. But the last stop on the line was in the ass end of Brooklyn; it was a place that journalists and policymakers didn't report on or worry about. It was out there, not violent enough to be Brownsville or beautiful enough to be Fort Greene. Just a place where fingers trailed off the map, deeply disinterested.

D sat in the first car of the L train, his bags stacked on the seat next to him, wondering if revenge was ever actually sweet, cause mostly it felt like mourning with a smile.

CHAPTER 29
TIME FOR SUM AKSION

D stood in front of his office door, keys in his right hand and a plastic bottle of water in the other.

He'd learned so much in Cali that his old surroundings felt somehow unfamiliar, like he was seeing the lobby, the elevator, and the hallway with new eyes. It was D's *Matrix* moment and it felt as unsettling as anything Neo experienced after taking that pill. He knew the answers now and it neither satisfied him nor gave him a feeling that justice had been served.

And then D was in the exact spot where Dwayne Robinson had died not too many months before. There was no mystery to the death anymore. He'd filled in the last spaces in that crossword puzzle. There was no sense of accomplishment, however, no smug glee at having solved the puzzle—if "solved" was even the right word. His friend had died to cover someone else's tracks, to cancel out the memory of acts concocted by a small group of self-important men. What could he do with this tale? Post it online was the most likely scenario. There it would live alongside tales of the Illuminati, MK-ULTRA, and the secret coding of the Roc-A-Fella Records logo. In other words, his story would be embraced by the deep conspiracy theorist, read for amusement by the slightly paranoid, and ignored as crazy shit by everyone else.

So he stood in the space where Dwayne's life had bled out and said a prayer for his soul and hoped the Lord already had him writing an additional psalm to the Bible, angel wings slightly tilted for just a touch of B-boy swagga.

D fumbled a bit with the door before realizing that other members of D Security had been in and out while he was in Cali and, apparently, had been careless in locking up. Just something to put on the agenda for the next staff meeting.

Another thing to add to that agenda was that the light had been left on in his office—a crack of it slid out from under his closed door. But when D entered the room, he found a well-built black man with braided hair, a red and green dashiki, and a Desert Eagle in his hand sitting behind the desk. If D looked like a linebacker, this gentleman was a fullback, and the two of them seemed destined to meet head-on in a football field some snowy December afternoon.

D actually chuckled when he recognized the face. "Damn," he said.

"Yeah," Malik Jones replied, "it's your office. You might as well take a seat."

Jones looked darker than in his photos (tanned from time in the Caribbean or Africa?), and fuller, like he'd been eating well and wasn't afraid to let his belt out a notch or two. There was even a hint of an accent in his voice—something black and foreign and decidedly affected.

"I didn't think it would come to this. Didn't think there would ever be any reason for us to meet."

"Things happen," D answered.

"Yes, they do."

"You been in the Caribbean?"

Malik smiled. "I'm at home wherever black folks gather."

"Yeah," D said. "Rikers Island. Compton."

"New Jersey."

"Is this about your wife?"

"I know you didn't kill her. But you got her involved."

"You mean I got involved *with* her."

"You got involved with her to find out about me, and that got Eric all concerned, and the fool did what fools do."

"That's bullshit. You killed her. You killed Amina. She would never have written that letter for anyone but you."

Malik's voice had been steady so far but real anger was building in him and starting to bubble over. "You can act all virtuous, but you protect the scum of the earth. You know I know."

"So it's all about guilt?"

D used his right foot to sweep across Malik's left ankle, causing him and the chair to spin sideways. Malik lost his balance and D lunged with both hands for the gun. Malik squeezed off a shot that whizzed past D's ear and exploded into the door behind him. As the two men wrestled atop the desk Malik pulled the trigger again, nicking D's left bicep and sending a spurt of blood back into Malik's eyes.

D recoiled, his left arm smoking from the hole in his black suit. Malik fell to the floor, his hands furiously rubbing his eyes. For a moment both men, damaged and fearful, tended to their wounds. Malik recovered first, his survival instincts sharp after years hiding in the shadows. He pulled himself from the floor and, through truly bloodshot eyes, spied the gun on top of the desk. He lunged for it with both hands, determined to fire a kill shot.

D reached up with his good arm, grabbed Malik by the scuff of his jacket, fueled by anger and adrenaline, pulled the man across the desk, and slammed him face-first onto the office floor. Two more shots flew from the gun, sending hot metal ricocheting off the floor and ceiling. One landed in the top of the desk. The other found a home in the fleshy part of Malik's right ass cheek.

The most dangerous weapon in any hip hop–era fight was not a left cross, an Uzi, or a box cutter. The things that inflicted the most damage were thick soles of Timberland boots and chunky athletic shoes. The stomp-down—brutal, relentless, and sure to crack bones and rip holes in important organs—was a weapon most lethal. And D applied it to Malik's body with gusto. He started on the man's hands, followed by his left shoulder, right knee, and, finally, his left cheekbone.

Malik, big and hard, was still conscious, but wished he wasn't. D pulled his office door open and then, using his right hand, dragged Malik's bloody, beaten torso through his small waiting room and doorway. He dropped the man inches from where Dwayne Robinson had lain dead not too long ago.

D looked down at Malik Jones, a.k.a. Anthony Jackson. The man was prone, dizzy, and fractured. The gun felt good in D's right hand. I can do this, he thought. There was no doubt. Not like Amos. The reasons were legion. His cause was just. Malik had killed a woman he cared for. The safety was off.

The staircase door suddenly opened and Sussanah, the yoga teacher from downstairs, peeked her head out into the hallway and took in the scene.

"D? D, are you all right?"

"I'm alive."

"I was in my studio. I heard the shots. The police are coming."

He looked back down at Malik. "I think you just saved me."

"Is he dead?"

"No, he isn't."

D engaged the safety and walked back into the office, put the gun on his desk, and sat on the floor, thinking maybe he should try to stop his arm from bleeding.

CHAPTER 30
EMPIRE STATE OF MIND

The yacht made a big circle in New York Harbor right in front of the Statue of Liberty. D stared at the illuminated torch and at Lady Liberty's steely gaze as he sipped on cranberry juice. The day's humidity had cooled into a temperate late-summer night and there was even a slight nip in the air with September just a few days away.

D shrugged his shoulder and smiled. Every day it hurt a little less. The doctors said he could hit the weight room right after Labor Day. There was only so much yoga a big man could do before he craved a forty-pound barbell in his hands. As the yacht moved past the site of the World Trade Center, D walked down from the top deck to see how things were going.

Jay-Z, Beyoncé, Chris Rock, Mary J. Blige and her husband Kendu, a pregnant Alicia Keys and her husband Swizz Beats were all chillin' at a long table, as they finished dinner and sipped on cocktails. D had ac-companied this illustrious group to Governor's Island for the Rock the Bells hip hop festival, which was highlighted by Lauryn Hill's return to a New York concert stage. It had been years since the revered and reclusive MC/vocalist had graced a Big Apple stage, and the royalty of contemporary black pop came out to pay homage.

As D stood back from the party and watched, he had the disturb-ing thought that if the boat went down with the three ladies in it, the entire last twenty years or so of R&B would sink with it. If push came to shove, D knew he'd dive and help Swizz Beats with Keys first, though he figured pregnant women would probably be extra buoyant. D, as was his custom, didn't try to eavesdrop on his clients, and what he did hear, he did his best to forget. The men at the table, most of whom were from Brooklyn, were telling tales of infamous stick-up kids, including the original 50 Cent.

Then someone mentioned the "plot against hip hop" and D, who'd been standing about ten feet away, suddenly found himself three feet from Chris Rock's chair. Someone had heard tell of an OG named Ice out in the Ville who'd "handled" a white man who "someone said" was involved with a group "trying to fuck up the game." Rock ran with this, riffing on the fact that artists like Soulja Boy were the biggest threat to hip hop since Vanilla Ice.

Quickly the conversation went spinning into why Lauryn Hill was the best female MC ever and which male MCs she was better than (which turned into a long list). To the celebrated folks at the table, the plot against hip hop was just entertaining dinner table conversation, something to smile about and then move on. D thought of Dwayne Robinson's unfinished book, which was just one more of humanity's unfulfilled dreams.

Yet it had been no dream. It had been as real as the knife wound to Dwayne's gut and the bullet hole in D's shoulder. He wanted to tell them all—the star MCs, the superproducer, the great divas—how true it was. But that wasn't his job. He protected people. At least that's what he aspired to do. So he looked over at the group, nodded at Jay (who nodded back), and headed up to the top deck to finish his cranberry juice. One side of the boat was the city. The empire state of mind in full effect. On the other was New Jersey, a place to which he now felt surprisingly tied.

He took a sip of juice and wondered how much he really knew about anything that had transpired these past few months. Had Amos Pilgrim told him everything? The old man had implied there were many situations he still had his hand in. And what about his cancer? That could have just been a bid for sympathy or a ruse to throw D off. Far as he knew, the old dog was a little bruised, but still alive out in Cali.

D had done his best to uncover the plot, but he knew he hadn't done much, and surely what he had done wasn't enough. He thought of the way MCs used the word *cipher*, which was a bunch of brothers in a circle rhyming. But a real cipher was a form of encryption, a word that hid the real meaning of things in plain sight. If you didn't know the references or catch the slang of an MC's rhyme, its real meaning could be as elusive as a dream. The words could be reworked to mean anything and everything, if the MC was skilled enough and the listener was committed to hearing.

As the boat moved slowly toward the dock at Chelsea Piers, D drank down the last of his juice and recommitted himself to hearing, listening, and understanding. He saw dock workers at the pier, a raft of expensive cars, and a couple of men with cameras in the far distance. He headed downstairs. Time to go back to work.